"What are you doing?" Madalena whispered in growing alarm

"Oh come, *ma belle*," said the Duke, slowly removing his coat. "Surely I don't have to spell it out—to you, of all people. I am assured that the French understand these things much better than the English."

"You are mad—or very drunk!" said Madalena. "Yes, that is it—you are drunk!"

"Very probably."

"Someone will miss me from the ballroom and come to look," she gasped, backing away as the waistcoat slipped from his arms and his fingers moved up to loosen his cravat. "I shall scream."

"No you won't," the Duke smiled, and as he calmly moved toward her, she felt the bedroom bureau hard at her back.

Madalena knew that in leading the notorious Duke of Lytten on, she had been playing with fire—and now she felt the fevered flames of passion rising to consume her body and destroy her good name. . . .

Big Bestsellers from SIGNET

MADALENA

by Sheila Walsh

A SIGNET BOOK

NEW AMERICAN LIBRARY

TIMES MIRROR

NAL BOOKS ARE ALSO AVAILABLE AT DISCOUNTS
IN BULK QUANTITY FOR INDUSTRIAL OR
SALES-PROMOTIONAL USE. FOR DETAILS, WRITE TO
PREMIUM MARKETING DIVISION, NEW AMERICAN
LIBRARY, INC., 1301 AVENUE OF THE AMERICAS,
NEW YORK, NEW YORK 10019.

SIGNET TRADEMARK REG. U.S. PAT. OFF. AND FOREIGN COUNTRIES
REGISTERED TRADEMARK—MARCA REGISTRADA
HECHO EN CHICAGO, U.S.A.

SIGNET, SIGNET CLASSICS, MENTOR, PLUME AND MERIDIAN BOOKS
are published by The New American Library, Inc.,
1301 Avenue of the Americas, New York, New York 10019.

First Signet Printing, May, 1977

1 2 3 4 5 6 7 8 9

PRINTED IN THE UNITED STATES OF AMERICA

Prologue: Sussex, 1812

THE MARCH NIGHT was wild. The small figure being buffeted along the path to the clifftop stumbled and threw out a hand to clutch at a tuft of coarse grasses, then ran on into the dark tunnel of trees, where the branches writhed in agony and twigs like clawing fingernails snatched at the heavy woolen jacket and snarled themselves in unruly curls.

The trees gave way at last to the wide sweep of headland just before it dipped into a deep, narrow gorge. The young face turned eagerly toward the open sea, fear struggling with a fierce exhilaration. Almost at once a light stabbed the raging darkness, and from the house set high at the apex of the gorge came an answering flash. It was inconceivable that anything could come ashore on such a night, for even above the howl of the wind could be heard the crashing surf below.

The young intruder stretched on tiptoe to peer further into the darkness, and a huge stallion, black as the night itself, loomed out of nowhere. It squealed and reared up; the rider swore viciously and dragged hard back on the rein, almost unseating himself and sending the instigator of the near-disaster catapulting into a ragged clump of gorse.

"Hell and damnation! Come out of there this instant and declare yourself!"

A small, bedraggled figure slowly emerged from the sodden gorse bush, brushing away dirt and twigs with impatient gestures and muttering Gallic curses of a fluency astonishing in one so young.

"Come here, boy!"

The moon, which had been scudding in and out of mountainous black clouds, suddenly sailed clear, silhouetting horse and rider in one enormous, frightening entity: huge flapping shoulder capes whipped about a face that was no more than a white blur beneath the high conical hat, and the stallion, showing white-rimmed eyes, backed nervously in an effort to escape the tight rein, and snorted little puffs of steam.

The child shrank back, convinced that, of a surety, it was the Devil himself.

The black rider leaned down from the saddle and hooked his riding crop beneath the miscreant's chin, jerking the head up; bright curls glinted in the moonlight, crowning an extraordinary monkeylike little face.

"Who are you, boy?" The question was rapped out—in French this time. "What mischief brings you here?" The riding crop prodded harder. "Come—I will have an answer."

Stormy eyes stared back at him in stubborn, unyielding silence—a silence that was never resolved, for cloud once more swept across the face of the moon, and when it cleared, the rider was alone.

He paused, irresolute, and in a momentary lull his keen ears picked up the sound of oars being shipped. He turned at once toward the sound, dug in his spurs, and urged the stallion forward to pick its way down the treacherous cliff path.

And in the darkness behind him, a figure emerged from the bushes and watched him go.

Chapter 1

LIGHT STREAMED FROM every window of the house in St. James's Square. Echoes of music and laughter drifted out on the night air, to be lost in the jingle and creak of harness, the clattering of carriage wheels, and the forcibly expressed opinions of coachmen as they maneuvered their already close-packed vehicles to make room for a late arrival.

In the brilliantly lighted foyer, two footmen sprang into instant action as the doors swung inward to admit a tall, saturnine gentleman.

In austere silence he relinquished his fashionably high-crowned beaver hat, his light walking cane, and the magnificently caped greatcoat; he adjusted the set of the plain black coat that already lay in unwrinkled perfection across the superb shoulders, and moved with an air of bored resignation up the wide, curving staircase toward the sounds of revelry.

"My Gawd!" The new, young footman stared after him in awe. "Who was that?"

"*That*, my lad," came the dry rejoinder, "is his grace, the ninth Duke of Lytten, of ancient and noble lineage—arrogant bastards, the whole Destain line, by all accounts, and this one don't aim to change the family image. Takes his women as he takes his wine—liberally, but with the palate of a connoisseur!" The old servant glanced around to make sure they were alone, and one eyelid drooped knowingly. "You'll be seeing quite a lot of his grace . . . if you take my meaning!"

The recipient of this doubtful testimonial had by now reached the head of the stairs, where a dark, restless beauty at once detached herself from a small group of exquisites with a laughing apology and came toward him, hands outstretched.

"You are late, Dev," she reproved sternly. "I declare I had quite given you up."

The duke carried her hands to his lips. His mocking glance moved with frank appreciation over the daringly cut soft green crepe gown that so exactly complemented her laughing eyes.

"But surely, my dear Serena, you knew I would come. When have I ever let you down?"

Lady Serena Fairfax drew him a little aside. "I knew nothing of the kind, you wretched man," she complained softly. "I did not even know if you were safely arrived home."

"Well, for that omission you must blame my lord Castlereagh," he murmured with some feeling. "I landed only this morning, and have spent the entire day closeted with him—and later with our beloved war minister, who must needs hear all again at first hand.

"I tell you, my dear, it was a marathon performance deserving of the very highest reward." His words were charged with a quite unmistakable meaning and drew a soft chuckle from his companion.

"Later," she promised. "When my guests have gone. We will be cozy, and you shall tell me all."

One calculating eyebrow lifted. "If that is all I am to hope for, I may well seek more . . . accommodating company!"

This threat was greeted with more mirth. "Poseur! Very well, you shall have your reward, but you must know I am impatient to hear about the war—and how Lord Wellington goes on."

For an instant the mask of ennui slipped, and he spoke with soft vehemence. "I have no doubt that our newly elevated earl is a great, a formidable commander! But I have just pursued him over half of Portugal, into the jaws of a hell called Badajos—a bloody experience, and such a one as I hope, by God's grace, never to encounter again! Yet I survived, and have returned to an eight-hour inquisition at the end of it." He shrugged. "I can do no more, my dear Serena—even for you!"

She looked distressed and would have spoken, but the mask was firmly back in place once more; a fat lady who would have approached them wilted under his intense stare and retreated in disorder. He sighed. "The company looks as distressingly boring as usual, my dear. I trust your card room is up to scratch?"

Lady Serena shook her head at him. "I positively forbid you to bury yourself in my card room until you have circulated a little among my guests. You know how much of a stir you create—how much it delights me to see all the fond mamas marshaling their dewy-eyed offspring for your approbation!"

His eyes glinted. "Someone should inform them that they waste their time. I'll wed no whey-faced infant; even in my dissolute and inglorious youth I ever preferred women of taste and experience!"

Lady Serena laughed. They had known each other too long and too well to dissemble.

"Well, do go and make their hearts flutter just a little. I promise I have done my best to afford you some small amusements."

"What are you plotting, Serena? You have a look I mistrust!"

"Nothing dreadful, on my word. It will shock only the prudes—and some of the straitlaced old dowagers!" Her eyes brimmed with mischief. "Lord Palmerston and I are to demonstrate the 'wicked waltz,' and we are fully expecting others to follow us on to the floor. You must find yourself a partner, for I will not believe you are not an expert in the waltz, as you are in all else."

His brow lifted sardonically. "You flatter me, my dear. But who is to match me, since you are bespoken?"

"My dearest Devereux, you know very well there is not a woman in that ballroom whom you cannot command, should you so choose!" The mischievous look was back. "Caroline Lamb is here—I am sure she would oblige you!"

"Caro Lamb would oblige anyone . . . anytime!" came the duke's pithy retort. At that moment Lady Serena's attention was claimed, and her husky laugh floated back to him as he raised his eyeglass and allowed his glance to wander slowly around the huge, gilded ballroom.

As always, Serena's guests seemed to include almost everyone who was anyone; for even those who disliked her, or perhaps had cause to fear her at-times faintly malicious tongue, accepted her invitations with alacrity. It was widely acknowledged that the Lady Serena "had influence"; her late husband had held high office in the government, an office in which he had been successful largely due to his wife's undoubted capacity for political intrigue. It was a talent she still put to good use whenever called upon so to do.

A cotillion was just coming to an end, and the couples began to disperse. A liberal sprinkling of uniforms lent vivid splashes of color to the already colorful scene.

Along the perimeter of the room a clutch of young girls sat chattering like a flock of birds—no, doves—he thought sardonically. A flock of virginal doves. He knew from the sudden spate of giggling and fluttering that his presence had been noted, and he sighed.

One corner of the ballroom seemed to be attracting a deal of lively attention. The duke trained his eyeglass upon the center of the group. A low, musical laugh floated out above the hum of conversation, and the young men pressed eagerly forward. Then, as though being dismissed, they began to drift away one by one, and he was left staring into an engaging little monkeylike face topped by a close-cropped head of bright copper curls. . . .

Madalena de Brussec turned impulsively to the pretty blond girl who was her cousin. "Phoebe, you will tell me please, who is the man who stands by the door—the one who looks like Satan. He will not take his eyes off me!"

Phoebe Vernon followed her gaze and let out a little gasp. "Lud, child—it's Lytten!"

"Should this mean something to me? This Lytten is a somebody?"

"The Duke of Lytten, my dear. His land marches with ours at home. In fact, he owns most of the land around us; his family have done so for generations."

Madalena's straight little nose wrinkled. "He is perhaps what you would call a feudal lord?"

"Lordy, what a thought! I suppose he is, in a way."

"So . . . you will know him?"

"No, hardly at all." Phoebe giggled. "He is a friend of Kit's, though he is considerably older—well into his thirty-fifth year, I believe." She giggled again. "He has the most dreadful reputation."

"Vraiment!" Madalena studied this wicked duke more closely. She met his raking glance with a speculative tilt of her chin; he smiled faintly and inclined his head in answer.

At Madalena's other side, a tall, willowy girl, with hair like a raven's wing, watched this exchange with obvious chagrin. Bettina Varley was an acknowledged beauty, and until Mademoiselle de Brussec's arrival in London, was used to being considered the most popular girl of the season. Yet Lytten had never looked at her in such a way. She could not imagine what people saw in the little

French chit with her cropped Parisian curls, but it was infuriating to be cast into the shade by one so frankly ugly! This was not strictly true, for although in repose Madalena de Brussec's features were ill-balanced, they were lit from within with so much vitality and pure joie de vivre that one noticed only how the large, almond-shaped eyes glowed with amber fires and the too-wide mouth was always tilted up at the corners, to disappear, as it frequently did, into two delightful dimples.

Miss Varley said waspishly, "It is no use trying to engage his grace's attention, mademoiselle, for he comes only to tease us. He has no interest in *jeunes filles.*"

Madalena turned a long cool glance on her. "You think not? He has not, then, tried to ravish you—no?" She smiled kindly. "It is perhaps just as well, for you would not at all care for it. *Quant à ça,* the English do not understand these matters as we French do."

"Madalena!" Phoebe was scandalized.

Hot color had crept up under Miss Varley's skin, but she snapped her mouth tight shut against the temptation to reply.

"But it is true!" Madalena insisted with a roguish twinkle. She tapped one tiny gold pump thoughtfully. "It would seem to me that this so arrogant duke should be taught a small lesson."

Phoebe groaned. "Oh, Madalena . . . no!"

"I am sure I do not know what you mean," said Madalena innocently. "You are as bad as Tante Esmé."

Her cousin eyed her nervously. Mama would not like it if Madalena made a scandal. "Promise you won't do anything . . . indiscreet!"

A gurgling laugh greeted this impassioned plea. *"Voyons*—I believe he is coming across."

The duke had accosted Kit Vernon, who was making for the card room.

"Introduce me, my boy," he commanded, indicating

the object of his attentions. "Since she is with your sister, I infer she is the little French cousin?"

Kit regarded him pensively; already more than halfway under Madalena's spell, he felt a swift, instinctive desire to protect her.

"I ain't at all sure I should," he said bluntly. "You've got that infernal gleam in your eye."

"As you will," drawled the duke. "I certainly don't propose to furnish you with a catalog of my intentions. Serena will, no doubt, be happy to oblige me."

"That damned haughty air don't cut no ice with me; I've known you too long." Kit grinned suddenly. "Oh, very well, I'll do the honors, but for God's sake watch it, Dev— I know she's a devilish taking little thing, but do try to remember she's family! Mama is already finding her a mixed blessing!"

"That I can well understand—a twin, I think you said?"

"As ever was. Like two dashed peas, except the lad's a half-head taller and a touch less volatile. See—there's Armand, talking with young Merchent."

A casual glance confirmed Devereux's suspicions, and he smiled.

The two men crossed the ballroom floor shoulder to shoulder, and Madalena watched them with frank interest. They were both well-built, but next to Kit's sandy fairness, this duke was more than ever sinister in his stark black, with only the white at his throat for relief; a single diamond pin glittered in the elaborate folds of his cravat.

The face seemed strangely familiar. But . . . yes, there was a picture of Satan in the prayer book she had had as a child, with just such a face—high molded cheekbones and a hooked nose with deep-etched lines running down either side of a full, sensual mouth. And the eyes! *Mon Dieu!* Such eyes. She shivered deliciously, remembering how she had feared that portrait.

When he stood at last before Madalena, she was able to

observe that the duke's eyebrows also had a curious upward flick, so that one might imagine them to be horns!

Kit perfomed his introductions. Phoebe blushed prettily and murmured something unintelligible, but Miss Varley, being included as one of the party, was much more willing to engage the duke's interest. However, beyond a brief nod, he paid her scant attention; his brilliant blue eyes were fixed with a curious intentness upon Madalena.

She returned the look with a complete lack of shyness and challenged in mock reproof, "Monseigneur le duc, you have been staring at me!"

He agreed imperturbably. "I hope you do not mean to take exception, mademoiselle, for you will have noticed that I am continuing to do so."

Madalena gurgled with delight, and Miss Varley's lips tightened visibly.

The waltz was announced, and amid a buzz of mingled excitement and disapproval, Lady Serena took the floor with Lord Palmerston.

Above the swell of the music, Devereux said abruptly, "Do you waltz, mademoiselle?"

"But of course, monseigneur. I regret, however, that I am already claimed."

"That can soon be arranged." He took her card and scanned it casually. "Ah, it's only Freddie Egerton." He turned to an eager young exquisite who hovered anxiously at his elbow, and bent a commanding eye upon him. "There you are, Egerton—you won't mind giving up your place to me, will you, lad?"

Without waiting for answer, he swept Madalena onto the floor, where some four brave couples were now dipping and swirling to the pulsating rhythm of the music.

"Freddie will not love you, duke," she protested breathlessly. "He has waited so patiently to show me his waltz."

"My heart bleeds for him!" he drawled. "Shall I restore you to him?"

Her huge, gamine grin flashed swiftly. "No, no, I beg you, for I am sure your performance is so much superior!"

Devereux laughed, and his arm tightened just a fraction, causing her to feel even more breathless. Madalena sighed, and abandoned herself to the ecstasy of being whirled around in strong arms.

"You are very masterful, are you not?" She sighed.

His eyes glinted down at her. "And you are a most provocative young lady. Tell me, mademoiselle, do your partners always have to wait in line for the favor of a dance with you?"

Madalena chuckled. "They are just silly boys. It is that I am French, you understand. I think they all mean to be in love with me, but it will not last, for I am not a great beauty or a wit, even!"

It was said without guile; was she, then, so totally unaware of her own attractions? Devereux accorded her the benefit of any doubt as she presently whispered with unholy glee, "See how the dowager ladies frown upon us! Is it that they consider me too *jeune fille* to waltz with such panache?"

"Very likely," he said, amused. "Though the waltz itself is sufficient to sour their humor—it is still frowned upon by some of the Patronesses of Almacks, and theirs is the criterion by which all such social niceties are judged. Have you visited Almacks?"

"No. One must have vouchers, you know. Tante Esmé hopes to obtain them, and Phoebe speaks of it with awe, but in truth, it sounds a very dull place."

"It is—excessively dull, but obligatory if one would be fashionable."

"Then I shall not repine if we do not go! Perhaps," she persisted wickedly, "the dowagers frown because I am with you?"

"That is also entirely possible. Does their disapproval distress you?"

"No!" It was a too vehement denial. For a moment the

laughing mouth trembled, and then it firmed again. "Already there are many who shun me. Not everyone, you see, loves me for being French." She shrugged philosophically. "One cannot blame them."

One satanic eyebrow flickered upward in surprise. He said softly, "Yet I, mademoiselle, was impatient to renew our acquaintance."

Madalena stared, her hurt forgotten. "But we have not met. No! It is impossible that I should forget such a one as you!" she continued with amusing frankness. "It was perhaps my brother, Armand. We are very like."

"No. It was not Armand."

"Then you will tell me, please," she demanded, "where was this mysterious meeting?"

On an impulse he said, "Ride with me in Hyde Park tomorrow at midday—and I will tell you."

Madalena looked up, considering him through her lashes. "I do not at all believe you, and I do not think that I *should* ride with you. Tante Esmé would undoubtedly consider you not at all a respectable person for me to know."

She became aware that the music had come to an end and that everyone was leaving the floor. "Monseigneur le duc!" she entreated. "People are staring. Please to take me back!"

The duke tightened his hold and smiled down at her in *such* a way! "At midday," he repeated softly. "Your promise, mademoiselle?"

"Yes . . . yes!" she agreed in a panic. "I will come!"

"Good." Imperturbably he escorted her across the now deserted ballroom floor, watched by the entire assembled company.

"See what you have done!" Madalena muttered. She walked very straight, trying not to blush. "It would serve you very right if I did not come tomorrow."

"But you will. Your curiosity will not allow you to stay away."

They had by now arrived back beside a speechless Phoebe.

The duke took Madalena's hand. "You do not play fair, duke," she reproached him with a rueful grin.

"Oh, hardly ever, my dear!" He raised the hand to his lips. *"À bientôt.* Your servant, Miss Vernon."

Lady Serena was waiting in the doorway to steer him away from the card room. She linked an arm casually through his, and her laugh trilled out as she chided him good-naturedly. "Dev, you are a fraud! After all your protestations, you laid siege to our little *émigrée*—a positive babe!"

"Ah, but one, you must admit, who is quite out of the common!" he murmured with the faintest glimmer of a smile. He realized he was being maneuvered into a quiet corner, and added quizzically, "Why are you abducting me, Serena? Did I not know you better, I might imagine you to be jealous."

Lady Serena's manner became a little abstracted; she appeared to be examining minutely a mammoth arrangement of spring flowers. "You have a visitor," she said quietly.

The duke's expression hardly altered. "Leclerc?" he muttered.

She nodded.

"Damn him for a fool!" he exploded softly. "Has he no more sense than to show himself here when the house is full of people?"

"I gathered it was urgent. He was not seen, except by my servants—and they know how to be discreet. I have had him shown into the small back parlor, but you had best go to him directly, or he will work himself into a state!"

The duke descended the staircase without apparent haste. He waved away the two footmen who sprang forward at his approach, and walked to a door at the back of the hall.

As he opened it, a taut figure—slight, with a pallid face, curiously scarred—paused in the act of pacing the floor and threw up his hands in a torrent of French.

"*Taisez-vous!*" the duke rapped out in a voice that Madalena would have instantly recognized. "Do you wish to lay all we have worked for in ruins?"

Chapter 2

MRS. VERNON LEANED her throbbing head against the faded squabs of her brother's town carriage. She reflected bitterly that her sister-in-law, for all her high-toned notions, was as niggardly as Roger in the matter of his carriages, or she would have long since persuaded him to replace this badly sprung vehicle with something more stylish. A particularly ill-rutted patch of road confirmed her opinion and set her head pounding afresh.

A burst of stifled giggling from the opposite corner roused her. "Do stop whispering, girls." She sighed gently. "Madalena, dear child, I do not wish to appear . . . unfeeling, but I must tell you I think it most unwise of you to encourage a man of Lytten's reputation. I declare I did not know where to look this evening! I could only be thankful that Lady Fleet was unable to accompany us, though she must surely get to hear of what happened. Your behavior was, no doubt, due to ignorance of our ways, but though the duke is in some sort a friend of Kit's, he can in no way be considered a suitable companion for a young and innocent girl."

More giggles were hastily smothered, and from the

darkness came a short burst of coughing, followed by Armand's lazy drawl.

"Tante Esmé, I regret you waste your words. My sister will do as she has always done—exactly as she pleases."

"Oh, dear!" Mrs. Vernon was beginning to feel a little out of her depth with these odd, unconventional children, so unlike her own family. Of course, Kit resided almost permanently in London these days and was thus beyond parental restraint, but to be sure, he had always been a dear good boy; and certainly the girls, both Louise, now married and a mother herself, and her little Phoebe, who was betrothed to the charming son of an old friend, had neither of them ever caused her a moment's unease.

She did hope that these two children of her poor departed sister, who were proving so . . . unpredictable, would not be an unsettling influence for Phoebe. Of course, they were dear children, and one was very fond of them, but it was so uncomfortable not knowing quite where one was with them.

Mrs. Vernon supposed vaguely that it all stemmed from their losing their mama at a crucial age, and having a father who not only was French but also had strong radical leanings; everyone knew what excesses *that* combination could produce!

To be sure, Etienne de Brussec was a man much respected in France. A lawyer and a man of letters, he had served that creature Bonaparte faithfully for years; but of late he had become a stern critic of his emperor and of the policies that were plunging the country he so loved into ever more useless wars.

Since he was not a man to wrap up his opinions, his position had grown steadily more insecure. Only his immense popularity with the common people had so far stayed Bonaparte's hand, but he was constantly spied upon, and stood in imminent danger of arrest.

One might have supposed, Mrs. Vernon reflected irritably, that such danger would give him pause for thought.

But no, his only concern was for his seventeen-year-old twins; Armand in particular had a delicate constitution, and only a tiresomely long illness had so far kept the boy from being drafted into the army. As soon as he was sufficiently recovered, it became imperative to remove both children to the safety of their English relations.

Of course, Esmé Vernon had not refused Etienne's appeal for help; indeed, it never entered her head to do so, for she was a kindly woman. Her husband, the brigadier, was roused from the writing of his memoirs long enough to make all the necessary arrangements, and the twins were smuggled out of France—reluctant and protesting.

In Sussex they had seemed quiet and well-mannered, if a trifle . . . different, a trait she had attributed to their being in a strange country. It had seemed a good idea to coerce her brother into accepting some measure of responsibility for their entertainment, and an invitation was finally wrung from him to bring them to London for a short stay to celebrate their eighteenth birthday.

Viewing it now, in retrospect, their aunt wondered that she had felt no presentiment of impending disaster, for already, after only two weeks in London, Madalena was proving to be somewhat of a handful, exhibiting a degree of vivacity she had never shown in Sussex. And now, there was Lytten!

There were few people taking the air on the following day when, at a little before noon, Kit Vernon rode in through the park gates in company with his sister, Phoebe, and his two young French cousins.

Phoebe, let into the secret, cast surreptitious glances about her, eager to discover if the duke would come, while Madalena displayed a masterly unconcern.

She kept up a seemingly endless stream of small talk and exhibited just the correct degree of surprise as his grace was seen approaching mounted upon a spirited black hunter. Kit shot her a suspicious glance, which she met with limpid innocence.

Greetings were exchanged, and Armand was introduced to the duke. Under cover of the ensuing conversation, Kit leaned across to his friend.

"I have the distinct feeling that I have been used," he murmured. "Am I right?"

Devereux's expression was bland. "How should I know, dear boy?" He wheeled his horse around in order to ride along with them. By degrees he contrived to fall a little way behind with Madalena.

"You come well chaperoned, mademoiselle," he observed dryly.

"But of course. You did not expect that I would come alone?"

He turned to look at her. She wore a riding dress of deep brown velvet, its short jacket curving neatly into her tiny waist, the sleeves tight and braided; her high-crowned shako sported a dashing peak and a feather curling bewitchingly over one ear; pale yellow kid gloves completed an outfit that was completely at odds with the way he had first seen her.

"And does Mademoiselle de Brussec always do what is expected of her?"

The tone of his question made her glance up sharply. "Why do you say this?"

"Because I know she does not," he said softly.

The curled plume bobbed as she tossed her head. *"Tiens!* Now you are again being mysterious!"

"May I applaud your excellent command of the English language, mademoiselle?"

Madalena's eyes twinkled suddenly. *"Merci bien,* Monseigneur le duc, but I did not meet with you in order to make polite conversation."

"No?"

"No. And if you have constrained me to ride with you

here only to tease, I think it a most shameful and ungentlemanly thing to do."

Devereux was enjoying himself more than he would have believed possible. "Speaking of riding, mademoiselle, is that animal the best Sir Roger Fleet's stable could provide for you?"

Madalena laughed and leaned forward to pat the cob's thick neck. *"Doucement!* You must not insult Angus—he has a most sensitive nature. My uncle's wife, Lady Fleet, with whom we stay, considers him the perfect mount for a young lady." She sighed. "Ah, but he is not like my own dear Diable, who is at home in Plassy." She cast an envious glance at the duke's hunter. *"He* is much like your horse—not so large, of course, but with such spirit, such character. . . ."

"You did not find my Thunderer's character so endearing at our last meeting."

Madalena jerked on the rein, and the cob stopped dead.

"Monseigneur le duc, I am quite *ennuyée* with all this talk of meetings, which I do not at all believe. I do not go any further until you explain it to me."

The duke's smile was gently mocking. "Then look well at my Thunderer, *ma petite,* and cast your mind back— a mere matter of weeks—to a stormy night . . ."

Puzzled and half-annoyed, she looked—and with the dawning of recognition her eyes grew wide. A stallion black as the night . . . rearing up before her . . .

She let out a little shriek and clapped a hand to her mouth. Ahead of them Kit turned, wondering if something was amiss.

"Mon Dieu!" breathed Madalena. "You are *that one?"*

The duke inclined his head. "And I'll lay a monkey," said he, "that your aunt had no idea you were wandering the cliffs so late—and in such unseemly garb."

She had the grace to blush. "They are breeches Armand had outgrown. I wore them often at home when we went exploring together. Now he is older, he is grown too grand for such adventures."

"But not you? You were not afraid of the storm?"

"Oh, no! I like storms." Her eyes shone. "I think sometimes I like to be frightened a little. And then, there were the lights, you see."

"Lights? What lights?"

"The smugglers' lights from the sea."

His voice sharpened. "You have a vivid imagination, mademoiselle!" And with an air of finality he added, "You would do well to keep off the cliffs at night in future. It is not safe."

"I do not imagine!" Madalena retorted indignantly. "How like a man to say so. And what should not be safe, unless . . . but yes, I have it!" In her excitement she prodded the cob sharply with her booted feet, and the startled animal almost broke into a canter. "Now I know why you were so angry that night! I have discovered your secret, monseigneur!"

"Have you, indeed?" The duke's voice was without expression. "And what, pray, *is* my secret?"

"Why, that you are a smuggler!" When he did not reply, she rushed on, "I shall not tell anyone, but I am right, am I not? Oh, I should have guessed it at once, only that you do not look like one!"

He met her long, considering look with coolness. "And how does Mademoiselle de Brussec imagine a smuggler should look?"

"But I know, for the men who brought us out of France were smugglers, I am sure—and they were rough, uncouth men!" Her nose wrinkled at the memory. "In the middle of the sea they met with a British Navy frigate"—she brought the words out with a flourish—"and we were taken on board without question! It was most odd, but *fort amusant,* you know."

Devereux laughed suddenly. "What an extraordinary girl you are!"

"Do you think it?" Madalena sighed. "Then it must be so, for Tante Esmé also finds me strange."

"You must not refine upon it too much, child—it will take a little time to adjust. I suspect you are missing your home."

"I am missing Papa," she said in a flat little voice. "And I worry about him. We did not at all wish to come to England, Armand and I. Oh, for Armand perhaps it was necessary; he has a weakness of the lungs, you know; it is a great trial to him, and he hates anyone to speak of it. But I know Papa feared for his life if he was taken for the army."

Madalena looked up, and there was a mutinous set to her mouth. "But if Papa is in danger, then I at least should have remained with him."

"Is your father in danger?"

"I very much fear it. To understand, you must first know Papa."

"I know of him," Devereux said. "Is he not one of France's most able and respected lawyers?"

She threw him a shining glance. "Oh, yes! And the people love him dearly. They know, you see, that his opinion cannot be bought."

"And yet he is in danger?" The duke found his interest caught and held by this child who held her father in such high esteem. He had heard rumors of De Brussec's outspokenness.

"It is the emperor," Madalena confided, echoing his thoughts. "No one has supported him more staunchly than Papa—indeed, in the early days he was one of his principal advisers. But in the last two or three years, Papa's counsel has been constantly rejected. Napoleon Bonaparte, it seems, is now so great he does not need advice."

The words were spoken with bitterness. "And since Papa will not stoop to dissemble as others have done, since he makes plain his views, he falls ever further from favor. Now there is this talk of a march against Moscow, and many more thousands of men and boys are called for the army. Papa will not be silent—and our emperor is not renowned for his patience . . ." her voice trailed away miserably.

"And so he sends you away?"

Madalena brushed an impatient hand across her eyes. "Yes, monseigneur—and I very much fear that when the emperor learns of it, he will be further enraged."

Devereux said with deliberate matter-of-factness, "You are singularly well-informed about your country's affairs, mademoiselle."

It had the required effect. Madalena said with some of her old spirit, "Lady Fleet would not think it becoming in a girl, I am sure, but Papa has always encouraged us to take an interest and to question everything. It is not easy here, for Tante Esmé says 'Yes, dear,' but she does not really listen, and the brigadier thinks only of his memoirs."

She grinned suddenly. *"Eh bien,* I am growing morbid. It is not *so* bad, for I have Armand . . . and Phoebe is very nice, I think, and in truth, I am having a splendid time in London. It is only, sometimes . . ." There was a fierce look in her eye, a determination not to give way to her feeling of desolation. "Papa will not write . . . we do not expect it, but to know nothing . . . to say nothing— it is not easy."

"You may talk to me, if you wish," Devereux offered unexpectedly. "I cannot pretend I have ever visualized myself as a father figure, but . . ."

Madalena gurgled irrepressibly. "You will perhaps discover a hidden talent!"

"Who knows?" he agreed with a faint answering smile. "And now I think we must join the others. Kit is throwing us black looks."

They broke into a canter, and as they rode several heads

turned in surprise to see the arrogant duke in such unlikely company.

"You must visit my mother when you return to Lytten
Tracy."

Madalena turned on him a look of pure astonishment,
and when he queried its cause, she confessed, "It is that
one does not think of you with a mother."

Devereux eyed her quizzically. "Your opinion of me
is now distressingly revealed, mademoiselle. But I assure
you I did not materialize one night in a thunderclap."

She chuckled.

"Unfortunately, my mother does not have good health."
His voice had changed so abruptly as to be almost un-
recognizable. "She is now wholly confined to the house."

"Oh, that is sad!" At once Madalena's warm heart was
stirred.

"Yes," he said. "She too is French. I think you would
like each other."

"Then of course I must call. I should, of all things,
enjoy it!"

It was only much later that Madalena realized the duke
had never really answered her query about the smuggling.

Chapter 3

"I AM SURE I don't know what to do for the best." Mrs.
Vernon's round, amiable face was pinker than usual and
creased with concern as she peered shortsightedly into the
severe countenance of her brother's wife. "One must rule

out coincidence. Wherever we choose to go, Lytten is there. Madalena is scarcely out of his company!"

"You should have adopted a much stronger line at the outset, Esmé." Lady Fleet's black bombazine skirts rustled ominously. "The familiarity between them at the play last evening was a disgrace! It is bad enough that we must endure publicly the spectacle of William Lamb's wife cavorting with that disgusting poet—"

"Oh, no, Hortense! You cannot compare Madalena's case with Lady Caroline Lamb's. To be sure, Lytten is no Lord Byron. I believe he sees Madalena simply as an engaging child."

"Hmp! You were always a gullible creature, Esmé." Lady Fleet was a stiff, angular woman, used to ruling her own family with an implacable will. "As I see it, you have only one course: you must forbid the connection. You stand, as it were, *in loco parentis;* the child is therefore bound to attend to you."

Mrs. Vernon wished she could share her sister-in-law's confidence. All very well for Hortense to lay down rules for her own family, but then, Roger had always been as wet as a pea-goose, even as a child—and their offspring, still at the schoolroom stage, were an insipid set with not an ounce of spirit among them.

She said with a touch of asperity, "It is not so simple, Hortense. The duke is our close neighbor. I am quite well acquainted with his mother—a dear creature and an invalid. To give offense could cause embarrassment. He has, after all, behaved with perfect propriety—one cannot say otherwise. What reason am I to offer to Madalena?"

Lady Fleet expressed astonishment that Mrs. Vernon should feel obliged to offer reasons. "Surely the duke's reputation is sufficient reason," she stated in her thin, hard voice. "Though your word in itself must be reason enough."

"Not, I fear, where Madalena is concerned."

Her ladyship oozed disapproval. "You know my views on *that* head. Those children have been shockingly over-indulged! The girl in particular. To educate a girl so highly is a dangerous, sinful waste; it positively encourages the worst excesses of vanity and argumentative-ness—indeed, I should be surprised if it does not, in fact, breed outright rebellion! I believe their father to have been much at fault!"

These strictures impelled Mrs. Vernon to rush at once into a defense of her niece and family. "At least, I do not have to worry about Armand—aside from his health, that is. He has become friendly with that nice Merchent boy. He is just enough older to be a steadying influence."

"I suppose Mr. Merchent must be considered quite un-exceptionable," the thin voice droned on. "His connec-tions on his mother's side are impeccable—she is a Norton of Brantwell, you know. He will inherit a considerable fortune there one day. I seem to recall some hint of scandal concerning his father, but of course, he, too, was French!" Lady Fleet's tone managed to convey that any flaw in the unfortunate man's character stemmed entirely from his unhappy accident of birth.

Mrs. Vernon, by now out of all patience, suddenly discovered a pressing engagement elsewhere.

It would have astonished her to learn that the duke in some measure shared her doubts about his suitability as a companion for her niece; indeed, nothing had been further from his thoughts at the outset. Madalena's mid-night escapade had certainly aroused his initial interest, but when they met again, he thought her an amusing child—no more.

And yet he found himself drawn back again and again to this half-child, half-woman who was so incredibly worldly wise for her years. He had no illusions about women, and had used them quite dispassionately as and when it pleased him, finding few, with the exception of

Serena Fairfax, who did not bore him to distraction within a very short space of time.

But Madalena was different. He found her witty, intelligent, and well-read; he enjoyed her company, enjoyed drawing her out, sometimes to the point of passionate argument.

To Madalena he was *grand seigneur* and teasing companion; she was soon so much at ease in his company as to be without any guile. She had long since abandoned any ideas of teaching him a lesson.

Kit Vernon was worried. He could see the way things were heading, and he knew his friend. But when he tried to warn Madalena, she only patted his hand and said serenely, "You are very kind, dear Kit, but you must not worry about me. I know very well what Dev is like, for I am not a fool."

It was true that she did not always understand Devereux. There was a dark and secret side to him that would not be drawn out—like the day in the park when they were all riding, and a strange, thin little man had attempted to engage his attention. He had been in a cold rage and had signaled for them all to ride on while he remained behind.

Madalena was sure that he knew the man, and the odd few words that floated back to her were in her own tongue. It had troubled her greatly, yet when she had later ventured a query about the incident, Dev had cut her off quite curtly and changed the subject.

But mostly he was teasing and indulgent, and the days slipped by until there were only a few remaining—and one of these was to be wasted upon a dull musical soiree to be given by one of Lady Fleet's cronies, Mrs. Arbuthnott.

The rooms were already crowded when they arrived. Phoebe's fiancé, John Brownlow, had come up to town and was there to meet them. Madalena liked him at once;

he was of medium height and almost as fair as Phoebe, and he had a nice smile.

Madalena had resigned herself to an evening of boredom without Devereux; one could not expect him to attend such a gathering, even to indulge her. And yet, just before the music commenced, there was a stir in the doorway—and there he was, eyeglass raised to survey the scene, while a flustered hostess rushed forward to greet him.

Lady Fleet, incensed by his unwelcome presence, went to great lengths to keep Madalena away from him, a piece of interference that did not sit too well with Mrs. Vernon, who considered herself quite capable of chaperoning her charge.

During one of the intermissions in a tedious program, however, Lady Fleet intercepted a wry exchange of glances between Madalena and the duke, and decided that more positive action was needed. This came in the form of Lord Ponsford, a godson of her mama's, who had most earnestly solicited an introduction to Madalena.

Lord Ponsford was not above five and twenty, but he seemed much older; already he was developing a paunch, and he worried incessantly about his health.

"Do not dare to leave me alone with him!" Madalena beseeched her cousin.

Try as they might, however, they could not shift his lordship, and at the end of the intermission he informed Madalena that he would be pleased to sit beside her if she should like it, and he could then extend to her the full benefit of his quite comprehensive knowledge of the works to be performed. There was no escape, and Phoebe and John led the way back into the concert chamber. Madalena insisted that they sit near the back, having seen Lady Fleet and Mrs. Vernon already seated on the front row.

"You are indeed fortunate, mademoiselle, to be invited to a concert of *such* quality!" Lord Ponsford was uttering in hushed tones.

Madalena turned her uncompromising stare upon him. "Oh, do you think so, Lord Ponsford?"

"Indeed yes, dear young lady. The soprano we are hearing is very fine—very fine. My music teacher used to tell me I had almost perfect pitch, and I can assure you that Miss Adelina Rossi is quite superb."

Madalena glanced about her in despair and saw Devereux leaning against the rear wall. He raised an eyebrow in mock sympathy.

"I make no doubt you are finding this a great treat," the silly man bored on, occasionally lapsing into very bad French. "The cultural life of your poor country must have suffered much in that dreadful revolution—and now, of course, you have that uncouth Corsican upon the throne."

Mon Dieu, no! This was too much! Madalena turned in her seat. "You are quite mistaken, monseigneur," she said in a flat voice. "Our culture is of the very highest— and far superior to this, I may tell you!"

Lord Ponsford gaped.

As the pianist played a cadenza and the large, full-bosomed soprano prepared to regale them once more, she whispered wickedly, "And I will also tell you, monseigneur, that me—I do have perfect pitch, and I say that woman's voice is flat. And now I am going into the conservatory, because it has suddenly become much too hot in here."

She stepped past him before he could recover his senses. Phoebe stared, horrified, and several heads nearby turned with curiosity or irritation as she walked quickly through the doors at the back of the room.

Devereux watched her departure with a gleam of amused admiration. After a few moments he followed her out and closed the door quietly behind him.

He found Madalena sitting dejectedly beside a giant flowering shrub, gazing into a fountain where a brightly colored tail fin flashed occasionally, picked out in the light flooding through the windows of the music room.

The disembodied voice of the soprano echoed on the scented air.

Devereux watched her in silence for some moments before chiding gently, "You are unhappy, *ma mie?* You have surely not fallen out with your gallant beau?"

Madalena's head shot up, and he saw the glint of angry tears.

"Parbleu! Do not speak to me of Lord Ponsford! He bores me to death with his delicate constitution, which does not in the least concern me, and with his talk of music, of which he knows nothing. Do you know, he thinks my people are a race of savages, and yet he has the impertinence to practice his atrocious French on me!"

"Dear me! You *have* taken against his lordship! That's a pity. I believe Lady Fleet was considering him as a possible suitor for your hand. He is very wealthy, I'm told."

Madalena sprang up in alarm. "No! This is not possible!" Too late she glimpsed the laughter in his eyes, and flew at him.

"Hush, little one!" He held her off. "Do you want to bring Lord Ponsford down on us? He may feel obliged to call me out."

"Peste!" An expression of horror crossed her face, and then the huge grin flashed out. "Oh, but you are wicked!" she whispered. "Always I say I will not allow you to tease. I mean to stay quite calm, and then—poof!" She threw up her hands.

He ruffled her curls. *"Couleur de diable!"* he murmured. Her face was turned up to him, and the diffused light lent her mouth a tantalizing allure. His fingers stilled and spread to cup her head. Without taking his eyes from hers, he slowly bent and kissed the softly parted lips, feeling an immediate leaping response.

He raised his head at last and said in a carefully controlled voice, "That should never have happened—I am sorry."

"I am not." Madalena smiled a small, secret smile. "I very much enjoyed it."

"Nevertheless, it won't do!"

She chuckled and slid her arms up around his neck, touching his hair where it swept in elegant wings from his face. "I had not noticed until now—there is silver in your hair. It gives you a look most *distingué!*"

"It is proof that I am too old for you," he said sharply. He endeavored to pull her hands down, but she only locked them tighter. "Stop it, Madalena! Be sensible, for God's sake!"

Her eyes were alight with laughter—and with love. "Oh, pooh! Me—I do not care for very young men. They are silly and *gauche!*"

"They are also more fitting companions for you," he reasoned, despairing. "You are too acute an infant to be ignorant of how I have used my years. I am not for you, my dear."

"But yes—I understand very well," Madalena insisted gently, "and I would not have you any different, my dear friend! And now you may kiss me, for I must return to that awful concert before Lord Ponsford comes looking for me."

Devereux groaned and swept her into his arms. This time there was nothing gentle in his kiss; he crushed her savagely to him, and she responded with a depth of passion that astonished him.

At last she gasped breathlessly, "I must go—but, oh, I do not want to! I would so much rather stay here with you. You *will* be at Lady Sefton's levee tomorrow?"

Devereux now had himself well in hand. "I shall be there, God help me! But if you look at me like that, I shall carry you off on the spot!"

All the way home in the carriage, Madalena endured a long tirade from Lady Fleet, who had discovered the whole of her disgraceful conduct; not content with slighting Lord Ponsford, a young man of irreproachable gentility, she had deliberately flaunted her assignation with that rake, that libertine. On and on she ranted, while Phoebe cringed; but Mrs. Vernon, observing her niece closely, was dismayed to find that she sat serenely oblivious, hardly hearing a single word.

At home in her room, Phoebe was bursting with curiosity, but found her cousin, for once, strangely reticent.

"But what happened, Madalena, in the conservatory?"

"Oh, we talked . . ."

This did not satisfy. Phoebe's eyes widened. "Did he . . . kiss you? Oh, Maddie, what was it like?"

Recollection curved Madalena's mouth in a dreamy smile. "It was like . . . Oh, I cannot describe!"

Phoebe, ever practical, foresaw trouble. "But what will happen? The duke is not . . . well, you know! Would your papa permit you to marry such a man, even supposing . . ." She stopped, embarrassed.

"Even supposing he wishes to marry me," Madalena finished the sentence for her. She shrugged her elegant little shoulders. "I do not for one moment think it, but it is unimportant."

"Maddie, you don't mean . . . ?"

Madalena laughed at the look of horror on her cousin's face. "Poor Phoebe. You find me very hard to understand, do you not? But to me it is very simple. If Dev asked me to go with him tomorrow, I would not hesitate. Does that shock you?"

"I don't know how you can even contemplate such a step," Phoebe whispered in awe.

Madalena patted her hand kindly. "That is how we are different, *chérie*. But do not let it distress you."

Lady Fleet was strongly of the opinion that for Madalena to attend Lady Sefton's levee was to court disaster, but Sir Roger, when appealed to, muttered vaguely that it seemed a great deal of fuss about nothing, and Mrs. Vernon, conscious of the distress such a ban would cause, stifled her qualms and for once agreed with her brother.

There was an added glow about Madalena on the following evening. Daniel Merchent noticed and remarked upon it to Armand, who glanced across the ballroom in surprise.

His sister was wearing her favorite dress—of silver-white gauze over satin, high-waisted, with little puff sleeves and floating panels. In the complete absence of jewelry, the only color was in the vivid, expressive face and short copper curls teased into a fringe across her brow. The result was a chic and stunning simplicity that many a more beautiful girl might envy without ever learning how to achieve.

To Armand, however, she was just his sister.

"Maddie? She looks well enough, I suppose."

Daniel Merchent raised an amused eyebrow. He was a pleasant, easy-mannered young man, well-dressed without any of the more flamboyant showiness of his other companion, a regular bang-up dandy.

Sir Vyvian Courtwell drawled lazily, "Marvelous, ain't it? The lad don't even see what a hot little filly his sister is; bit of a goer, too, so I hear."

Daniel frowned and shook his head as Armand looked from one to the other. "What is this 'goer'?"

"Take no notice, my boy," Daniel advised hastily. "Vyv is apt to favor the language of the turf." He added casually, "I confess, I should like to know your sister better."

"Then you must come to stay at Ivy Mount when we return to Sussex. Tante Esmé would not mind, I am sure."

"I should like that. She is very friendly with Lytten, I believe—your sister?"

"*Dieu!* Do not speak of it!" Armand grinned. "She has the aunts in a devil of a taking! They do not understand my Maddie very well, I think."

"Still, you can see their point," drawled Vyv. "I mean, Lytten ain't exactly a choice companion for a young girl."

"Oh, it is not serious, I think."

Madalena was puzzled when at first Devereux did not come, but she told herself that he was often late.

She did not really begin to worry until Bettina Varley minced across, looking more smug than usual.

"The duke has not arrived?" she inquired innocently.

"He will come very soon," Madalena replied with some hauteur.

The girl smiled. "I would not bank upon it, my dear mademoiselle. When I last saw him, he was very much occupied elsewhere."

"Please to say what you mean."

"I mean that as we passed Lady Fairfax's house on our way here, the duke had dismissed his carriage and was mounting the steps."

To cover the sudden sick fear in her heart, Madalena flared, "That is one big lie!"

Phoebe laid a warning hand on her arm, but it was swept away. "I know that you are simply jealous!" she added.

Bettina's lips tightened in anger, and then, as she looked toward the head of the stairway, her expression slowly changed. "Well! Who is the jealous one now?"

Madalena followed her gaze. Devereux was coming into the ballroom, and on his arm, laughing up at him, was Lady Serena Fairfax. Bettina's spiteful voice was full of ill-concealed elation.

"I declare I could laugh myself silly, Madalena de Brussec! You were going to be *so clever*—you were going to have Lytten at your feet. And now you are nowhere!"

The words went around and around in Madalena's head until it reeled giddily. She was still standing thus when Devereux's voice penetrated her misery. She stared up, uncomprehending.

"You are not paying attention, little one. I was tendering my apologies for being late. How many dances have you saved for me?"

Oh, the traitor! Such duplicity—to come straight to her from that woman, and actually smile!

"I regret, Monseigneur le duc," she said through stiff lips. "My card is quite full."

His eyebrow shot up in surprise, and then he laughed tenderly. "Well, we have overcome that difficulty before, *ma mie.*" He reached for her card, but she snatched it from him with trembling hands.

"You do not understand—I do not wish it changed!"

The duke's expression underwent a series of changes from disbelief and incredulity to cold fury.

"My God! Have you taken leave of your senses, Madalena?"

"*Au contraire,* monseigneur—I have just come to them."

His face would have frightened her if she had not been so overwrought. People were stirring uncomfortably; some watched with undisguised interest. In the silence, the music began to play, and Madalena's partner hovered nervously in the background.

Devereux turned abruptly on his heel, and then, seeing Bettina standing demure in victory, he stopped. There was an icy politeness in his manner. "Miss Varley, are you engaged for this set?"

Her eyes flashed a quick, triumphant glance at Madalena. "Only to my brother, your grace," she simpered. "I am sure he would be glad to give up his place."

Madalena watched them go, and her heart was slowly breaking in little pieces. The cool, husky voice of Lady Fairfax spoke at her side. "My dear child! Whatever are you about? You will never hold a man like Dev with those tactics!"

Madalena swung round slowly. "So? Doubtless you speak from your *very great* experience, madame," she said distinctly. "But me, I do not stoop to hold any man!"

It was so blatant an insult that Phoebe gasped, but

Serena Fairfax only raised an amused eyebrow and passed on her way with a light laugh.

Phoebe turned distressed eyes to John Brownlow and whispered brokenly, "Oh, Maddie! What have you done?"

"Done!" Madalena's laugh was shrill, and tears hovered on her lashes. "It is not what *I* have done!" She whirled around upon her by now apprehensive partner. "Why do you stand there? Can you not see I am waiting to dance?"

This wild mood of defiance sustained her for a while, and then, as it passed, she wished only to hide from the whisperings and the glances. She knew that she had made a bad scandal this time; Tante Esmé would be distressed, which made her sad, and Lady Fleet would have no more of her, which, even in her misery, concerned her not at all. But she could not face them yet.

She had been so sure that Devereux would leave, yet some time later his eyes found hers across the room, and their expression struck a chill of apprehension right through her.

Thinking only of escape, she slipped out of sight behind a small knot of people and moved swiftly to the nearest door, praying that no one would hinder her flight.

In the corridor Madalena hesitated, unsure which way to go. There was somewhere a retiring room into which they had been shown earlier—but where? Plunging to her left, she hurried along. All the doors were closed, and all looked alike. *Tiens!* This was absurd! Now, here was a corner and more passages! One look sufficed to show that Dev was on her heels, and panicking, she plunged again to the left and broke into a run. She must choose a room quickly. *Voyons*—there was a small recess ahead, and several steps up to a door. He had not yet reached the corner, and in a flash she turned the handle and was inside.

She leaned against the door to regain her breath while her eyes adjusted to the darkness. Silvery light filtered in through gently wafting muslin curtains, and soon she could make out shapes. There seemed to be an ornate daybed in the center of the room. So it appeared she was in some kind of boudoir.

Madalena stepped forward quietly, careful to avoid anything that might make a noise. Once a board creaked, and she froze, hardly breathing. When she was almost at the window, the door handle began to turn, and at once she slipped behind the heavy curtains. The door swung open, letting in a stream of light, and then after a pause, closed again, followed by the unmistakable sound of a key turning in the lock.

Peste! He had locked her in! Now what was she to do?

And then her heart stopped. There was a scraping sound—someone was lighting candles!

"You can come out now, Madalena," said the duke.

Disentangling herself from the curtain, she emerged, crimson with mortification. Devereux surveyed her with hard, glittering eyes, and she stared back defiantly. Neither spoke. Madalena glanced toward the door and saw that the key was gone.

"You have locked the door!" she accused him at last.

He removed the key from his pocket and let it lie in the palm of his hand.

"You will please to unlock it at once," she commanded with hauteur. "I wish to leave."

"Do you?" An unpleasant smile twisted his lips, and he returned the key to his pocket.

Madalena began to feel frightened. She did not know how to cope with this dark and dangerous mood.

"I . . . expected th-that you would leave," she stammered.

"Did you?" The voice was harsh, grating. "Is that how you imagined that it would be? That you, the little *ingénue,* would captivate the notorious Duke of Lytten, and then, when it pleased you, send him about his business while the world looked on? Oh, no, my dear—you picked the wrong man!"

"I don't know what you mean! I was simply enraged
that you were with 'that one' instead of me. . . ."

"We will leave Lady Serena out of this, if you please.
You have insulted her sufficiently for one evening!"

"I know," she confessed miserably. "I should not have
behaved so in front of everyone, but you know my temper
—how I do not stop to think!"

"Come now, Madalena—let us have an end to this
playacting. Wasn't it exactly as you planned it from the
very beginning?"

A cold fear was growing in her with every word, filling
her chest to suffocation and freezing the mutinous tears
behind her eyes.

"Can you deny that you set out deliberately to engage
my affections in order that you might cut me down to
size?"

"No!"

The cry was wrung from her aching throat, but the
cold voice went on, "I will give you your exact words, if
you wish. You were to 'teach me a small lesson.'"

Bettina Varley! Madalena could almost hear the sim-
pering voice artlessly dropping the words from her lips
like poisoned honey. "It wasn't like that!" she cried.

"No? What was it like? No—don't tell me. Explanations are tedious, and in this case, irrelevant; guilt, *ma
petite,* is written all over your so enchanting face."

Madalena shut her eyes. It was a nightmare; soon she
would wake, and it would not have happened. She pressed
her hands to her ears to shut out the remorseless voice,
but in a stride Devereux reached her and dragged them
down.

"What is wrong, Madalena?" he taunted. "Are you not
enjoying your triumph? For it *is* a triumph, my dear; you
have succeeded where all other women have failed!" The
voice hardened still further. "So. You have had your
pleasure—now it is my turn."

He thrust her away abruptly. Madalena watched in

horror as he began to remove his coat. She pressed a hand to her aching throat.

"Wh-what are you doing?" she whispered.

"Oh, come, *ma belle!* Surely I don't have to spell it out—to you, of all people! I am assured that the French understand these things so much better than the English."

In the heavy sarcasm, Madalena again heard Bettina's influence. How she must have enjoyed such a betrayal.

"No!" she said flatly. "I do not in the least wish to be ravished by you."

Devereux paused in the act of unbuttoning his waistcoat to eye her coldly and dispassionately. "Too bad, my dear; but the game has harsh rules, as you must have realized when you had the impertinence to involve yourself with me."

"I say you are mad—or very drunk! Yes, that is it— you are drunk!"

"Very probably."

"And you are also very stupid if you think to get away with this rape," she gasped, backing away as the waistcoat slid from his arms and his fingers moved up to loosen his cravat. "Someone will miss me from the ballroom and come to look. . . . I . . . I shall scream. . . ."

"No you won't." He began to walk toward her. With a sickening jolt, Madalena found a bureau at her back. The room had suddenly grown very hot, and yet she shivered.

"Trembling, are you?" he sneered. "Take heart, my dear Madalena—console yourself that in losing your virtue to me, you will at least be the envy of all your young friends, for do they not lie in their chaste little beds each night dreaming of just such a fate!"

"Dev, I implore you!" she sobbed brokenly. She would have given herself so willingly to the *cher ami* of last night, but this man with the face carved out of granite was a terrifying stranger, ruthless and single-minded. His eyes burned her up.

She put out her hands in a futile gesture, and then he

seemed suddenly to go very far away. Madalena was just aware of his astonished face before he vanished completely. . . .

Devereux was bending over her, his face very close. She was lying on the daybed, and as she struggled to sit up, he restrained her.

"Drink this first. Come, it is only brandy," he added dryly as alarm flared in her eyes. "Someone obligingly left it on the bureau."

"*Je ne comprends pas*—what has happened?"

"Nothing has happened, *ma chère* Madalena—except that you swooned away in a dead faint at my feet."

Madalena sat up abruptly, and for a moment her head swam. "Oh, but this is a great piece of nonsense! I have never swooned in the whole of my life!"

"Well, I assure you that you have done so now." His voice was tinged with bitter mockery. "Perhaps you have never had cause until now."

Madalena colored and stood up—too quickly. The duke put out a steadying hand, but she shook it off. "*Merci,* monseigneur, but I am quite well able to manage for myself."

In silence he took the key from his pocket and put it in her hand.

She stared at it, and then her eyes went to his face.

"You are letting me go?"

Devereux did not answer immediately; he was reliving the horror of that moment when she had sunk white and insensible at his feet—his utter revulsion with himself for what he had almost done. Nothing showed in his face, however, when at last he spoke.

"My dear child, you must know I have seduced a considerable number of women in my time; on occasion, I have met with some slight resistance." He paused, and again there was a hint of mockery in the hard, brilliant eyes. "But never until this moment has the prospect caused anyone to faint! And I find that nothing can be more surely guaranteed to kill all passion stone dead!"

He took the key from her nerveless fingers and crossed to the door.

Madalena followed as though in a dream. At the door she laid a tentative hand on his arm. "Dev, if you will permit me to explain? It was not the way it seemed. . . ."

At once his manner became withdrawn. "Leave it, Madalena," he said with harsh finality. "It is over."

She drew in a sharp breath, and without another word, and with her head held high to keep back the tears, she walked past him out of the room.

Chapter 4

Kit Vernon strode from the house and turned toward the stables, determined upon a brisk gallop to rid him of the black mood that had plagued him all the way from London.

Damn Lytten to hell! So arrogant, so damnably sure of himself as he was with all women, turning little Maddie's head with his smooth ways, and she, in spite of her confident assurances, not seeing that it was all a game.

Kit slashed the bushes savagely with his riding crop. It still rankled with him that he should be here in Lytten Tracy at all; he should be in London making Devereux answer for his conduct. He had missed the drama of the ball, but word had reached him soon enough, and he had rushed around to his aunt's, to find himself plunged into a most tremendous kick-up, with Mama and Phoebe in floods of tears, Uncle Roger ineffectual as ever, and Aunt Hortense, purple-faced and rigid with fury, declaring that nothing would induce her to house Madalena for one day further, that never would she forgive her for shaming them all before Lady Sefton and her friends!

When he had finally made sense of it all, nothing would do for Mama but that he should shepherd the family home to Sussex with all speed, and he, seeing Maddie standing there, deathly pale and stunned, could only agree.

Raised voices reached him as he approached the stable yard, and he rounded the corner to find Madalena there before him, berating the young undergroom soundly for refusing to saddle Perseus, the brigadier's big new hunter, which the lad steadfastly maintained would get the little mam'selle killed sure!

Kit eyed her stubborn face with its touch of desperation. "Jamie's in the right of it, m'dear," he said gently. "You can't ride that brute—he just ain't a lady's mount."

Madalena pointed a shaking finger toward a docile, waiting gray. "I will not have that sluggard, which can barely put one foot in front of the other when I wish to ride *ventre à terre*."

Kit hesitated, then quietly instructed Jamie to saddle another of his father's mounts—a bay mare with enough spirit to satisfy Maddie in her present mood.

While he waited for his own horse, he threw Madalena up into the saddle—and damnit, before he could draw breath, she had gathered up the reins and was away down the drive.

Kit swore mightily and cursed Jamie's fumbling fingers as they struggled with the girth straps. Then he too was away, pounding after her, trying not to remember that look in her eyes, not even sure which direction she had taken.

He came upon the horse at last, standing motionless in a clearing and Madalena bowed over its neck, lost in a wild frenzy of weeping.

Kit hung back, feeling a hopeless, inadequate anger in the face of such grief. At last the shuddering sobs grew less, and she sat up, her face blotched and swollen. When he spoke, his voice shook.

"If I'd known you were going to pull a cork-brained trick like that, I wouldn't have let you near that animal!"

"I wished very much to be dead."

"Well, you damn nearly succeeded! You scared hell out of me, I can tell you—I expected to come upon your mangled corpse at every turn."

Madalena put out a swift hand. "Poor Kit! I am sorry—it was not well done of me. I will not be so foolish again."

"I could kill Lytten!"

"Ah, but no—he is your *bon ami.*"

"Not anymore," he interposed harshly.

"What happened was not Dev's fault." She saw his look of patent disbelief. "Well, perhaps a little, but you do not know it all; I, too, behaved very badly."

"He had no business to engage your affections; he must have known what would be the outcome. If you remember, I tried to tell you."

"Eh bien, one cannot choose where to give one's heart." Madalena attempted a smile, but her mouth went awry. "If it gets a little broken, one must be patient and hope that it will mend."

She gave his hand a quick squeeze and straightened resolutely. "And now, we will ride back, and I think we will say nothing of all this."

Kit looked uncertain, and her eyes beseeched him. "Kit, I make you my promise. It is over! I do not wish your mama any further upset."

Kit shrugged. "Very well, m'dear—if that's how you want it, but I ain't happy about it. If you ever feel that way again . . ."

"I shan't."

And indeed, by the time Kit left to return to London, she seemed almost herself again, if a little quiet.

Her aunt was frankly puzzled. The quarrel with the duke must have left its mark, and yet the child resisted all attempts to speak of what had happened, even with Phoebe. There were no tears, no tantrums, no refusal to eat—though, to be sure, her appetite was ever tiny—nothing, in fact, that Mrs. Vernon would have considered normal in a young girl nursing a broken heart. It was just that one sometimes had the oddest sensation—as though a vital spark inside her had been snuffed out!

It was with some trepidation that she announced one morning to the girls that she was intending to drive over to Lytten Manor later in the day to visit the duchess.

Madalena's head came up slowly, a delicate flush staining her cheek. "Do you think . . . that is, would it be proper for me to visit with you?" The words came in a rush.

Mrs. Vernon stared, and hurriedly collected herself. "Why, of course you may, child—if you are sure?"

"Merci—then I will come." Later, in the carriage, Madalena queried with diffidence, "How is . . . Devereux's mama ill? I do not believe he ever said."

"I understand it to be a disease of the heart. She suffers a great deal—and with such patience!" Mrs. Vernon sighed. "It is quite tragic. She has a companion—a Miss Amelia Payne. She is a distant cousin of her late husband, a most pleasant woman, and devoted to the duchess."

The carriage had plunged into a tunnel of towering trees, through which the sun flashed in spasmodic dappled brilliance. The driveway climbed and meandered through luxuriant flowering shrubs, until suddenly they were out in the open. Madalena gasped, for it seemed they would drive over the edge of the cliff; then the carriage swerved sharply and in a moment drew to a halt.

Lytten Manor stood, rocky and obdurate, like a fortress, with its back to the sea, its grandeur softened only slightly on the landward side by the creeper that tangled obstinately upward, disguising its unlovely proportions. Unexpectedly, wildflowers burst between the flagstones in front of the door.

As they descended from the carriage, two large black retrievers ambled forward to put the visitors through a friendly inquisition.

A fresh-faced young footman ushered them into a massive, vaulted hall where quantities of dark oak paneling contrasted sharply with cool white walls. Logs blazed a cheerful welcome in the huge hearth, and there were flowers everywhere.

A tall, stooping butler came forward, and at the same moment a plump middle-aged woman in a round gown of blue muslin, with a charming matching cap on her graying hair, came hurrying down the wide stairway.

"Thank you, Gaston—I will look after Mrs. Vernon." Her eyes twinkled, and she held out her hands in greeting. "Mrs. Vernon—you are come to visit my dear Dominique. How kind! And this must be your niece?"

Madalena had been making friends with the dogs, but she stood up at once to be introduced.

"You are French—how splendid! Come, I will take you straight up. I must ask you not to stay too long, dear Mrs. Vernon. You will see how it is; Dominique tires so quickly now; Dr. Laidlaw has to be quite strict with her."

The duchess occupied a suite of rooms on the second floor, and Miss Payne led them into a vast blue-and-gold drawing room exquisitely furnished in the French style, across an endless expanse of rich gold carpet scattered with little sofas, gilded and upholstered in deep blue brocade.

From a chaise longue near the window came a softly accented greeting. Madalena tried hard not to stare, but found Dev's mama totally different from anything she had expected; indeed, it seemed inconceivable that life could exist at all in such a frail, emaciated frame.

Snowy white hair, stylishly dressed, and a rose-pink foulard peignoir, edged with swansdown and drawn high

at the neck, framed a tiny face, which, though ravaged
with suffering, must once have possessed a delicate beauty.
Only the eyes were vitally alive—bright blue, like her
son's, and burning with an unquenchable spirit. The smile
that greeted Madalena was of an incredible sweetness, and
something passed between them in those first few moments that was soon to forge a deep bond of affection.

As they talked, Madalena's eyes strayed constantly to a
nearby portrait. It was of a man—very *point-de-vice*—in
purple satin coat and much lace; one hand rested lightly
on the hilt of a dress sword, and about the eyes there was
a faint, mocking smile.

The duchess followed her gaze. *"Eh bien,* you are ad-
miring my Justin. Was he not a handsome rogue?"

"Dev is very like him, I think!"

The words were blurted out involuntarily, and at once
the duchess's glance swiveled around with a quickening of
interest.

"You know my son?"

A telltale flush had crept up under Madalena's skin;
she looked for all the world like a child caught out in a
misdemeanor.

Mrs. Vernon interposed hastily, "We met his grace in
London."

"But of course—how interesting! I had forgotten you
have been in London. You must regale me with all the
latest *on dits.* I confess I am ever eager for Devereux's
return so that he may bring me up to date on all the
scandals."

There was such a pregnant silence that the duchess cast
a quizzing glance from one to the other and surprised in
Madalena's eyes such a stricken look that she was moved
to exclaim quickly, "No matter—it will keep. My interest
stems purely from jealousy that I can no longer play my
part. And my wicked son is pleased to indulge me! Come,
we will talk of other things."

Mrs. Vernon's face expressed such patent relief that

the duchess was further intrigued, but she continued blandly, "Perhaps, Mademoiselle de Brussec, you will tell me of my beloved Paris—I expect I should find her much changed."

Madalena began to talk very quickly, and the moment passed, but before very long it became obvious that the duchess was tiring.

"I regret to be so tiresome." A wan smile curved the blue-tinged lips. She extended a woefully thin, yet still elegant hand to Madalena. "You will visit me again, *chérie?*"

"Merci," said Madalena shyly. "I should, of all things, like to come."

Her visits were soon a much-loved daily ritual. On the bad days, when breathing became a torture, Madalena would sit beside the vast canopied bed amidst shell-pink draperies, sometimes talking quietly of the mama she could scarcely remember and the papa she so adored, sometimes just sitting in a companionable silence.

A painting of the Madonna and Child on a nearby wall often drew her eye and moved her to confide wistfully, "I have a small alabaster statuette in my own room at Plassy. It is of the Madonna kneeling beside the Bébé's crib."

"You are missing your home very much, I think," the duchess guessed softly. "And your papa also?"

Sudden tears filled Madalena's eyes, but she blinked them back resolutely.

"Most of the time I manage. It is when things do not go well. Papa has a way of going straight to the heart of a problem, and at once it is made simple."

"And your dear aunt does not have quite this perception."

Madalena flashed her a quick, grateful smile. "Ah, you can see! Tante Esmé is a sweet, kind person, but one cannot talk to her. That is why I am so pleased that you permit me to visit with you."

Chérie, the joy is all mine! You have brought me a breath of something that I had almost forgotten. . . ." Their hands moved together instinctively on the silken coverlet, and Madalena could at once feel the febrile, uneven pulse.

"We will not talk anymore," she said quickly. "I will just sit here, and you may sleep if you wish."

For a long time they remained thus; Madalena allowed her thoughts to wander, until inevitably they turned to Dev. Soon he must return home. The mere possibility flooded her with an exquisite sensation of mingled joy and pain.

She became aware that the duchess was awake and regarding her all too expressive face.

"Tell me, child, that stricken look that I oft surprise in you—is my son responsible for that look?"

The convulsive tightening of fingers was answer enough.

"I would not cause you further pain, *ma mie,* but can you not bring yourself to speak of it?"

There was a vigorous shake of the head.

"Because I am his mama? Oh, child, I love Devereux dearly! He is to me a devoted son. But he is also a Destain of Lytten—and there is in all the Destain men a streak of ruthlessness, a degree of arrogance, especially in their attitude toward women. It can, unless they find a true and lasting love, mar their characters." She paused. "I very much fear you may have fallen a victim to this trait in my son's character."

With a stifled sob Madalena's head drooped. "No, no . . . it was entirely my own fault! I truly believe that he *did* love me . . . but something happened . . . I was stupidly jealous . . ."

"Ah!"

". . . I behaved very badly and made a scene at Lady Sefton's ball, with everyone looking on! And then . . ." There was an embarrassed pause. "And then . . . we had one big row . . . and all is over!"

The duchess stroked the fine copper curls, now spilled upon the coverlet. "Such finality, child? Devereux would be angry—that I can see—but he will perhaps forgive you, no?"

"I think not," came the muffled reply, "for he now believes that I am just a *coquette.*"

The duchess hid a smile and raised the tearstained face. *Voyons*—do you know, I had not thought my son so poor a judge of women!"

"N-no," stammered Madalena, coloring, "but . . . well, it is just possible that he had some cause . . ."

"I see."

"It was all nothing, but Dev was extremely angry." As she remembered, the light of battle flashed suddenly in her eye. "Which was most unfair, since he had behaved quite abominably and without the least regard for *my* feelings!"

"Ah! Then doubtless it is his pride that smarts! He feels betrayed—yes?"

Madalena nodded.

"Men! Always it is their pride! You must be very clever, *ma chère,* and show him that you are not repining."

"Do you think so?" Madalena sounded doubtful. "I was wondering if perhaps it is better that I do not come when . . . when Devereux is home. I would not wish for any awkwardness."

"You must do as you think best, child, but I should miss you." The duchess seemed suddenly exhausted, and Madalena was at once contrite and refused to discuss her troubles any further.

It was several days later, when Madalena had taken her usual shortcut across Lytten land and was about to step out onto the carriageway, that she heard a horse coming fast. Instinctively she shrank back into the shrubbery. The two dogs bounded ahead of Devereux on Thunderer. As they drew abreast of the place where she crouched, their heads came up, and with joyous yelps they veered off the road and came snuffling into the under-growth. She heard Dev wheel Thunderer around and call sharply to the dogs; their ears pricked, but they stayed panting at her feet, their tongues lolling with pleasure at this new and interesting game.

"Allez-vous-en!" she hissed. "Oh, please go, you great stupid animals!"

Dev's voice came again, nearer and more imperative. Peering through the leaves, she could see his topboots gleaming against the horse's steaming flanks. At the very moment that she had resigned herself to the ignominy of being discovered lurking in the bushes, the dogs reluctantly acknowledged the voice of authority and trailed their tails back to the road.

When the hoofbeats had quite died away, Madalena emerged, brushing a tangle of twigs from her dress, and stood uncertainly. . . .

The duke strode into the hall, stripping off his gauntlets and tossing them, with hat and riding whip, onto the nearest chair. Without pause he moved on up the staircase. At the door of his mother's room he checked, then knocked softly and entered.

"Devereux!" She held out eager hands, her bright eyes devouring him as he crossed swiftly to the bed. His heart stopped momentarily as he stooped to drop a kiss on each pallid cheek, and perceived at once her increasing frailty.

He settled beside her on the bed and possessed himself of her hand, a warm smile hiding his distress. *"Ma chère Maman!"* He used the affectionate greeting of his childhood. "How is my one and only love?"

The duchess chuckled and then sobered a little. "Am I still that, *mon fils?*"

"Oh, without a doubt, my dear; you are the only woman who has never failed me or in any way disappointed me." There was a hardness in his voice. She knew instinctively that he was thinking of Madalena, and she was about to speak when there was a soft rap on the door. It opened to admit Amelia Payne.

"May I come in, dear? Ah, cousin! Gaston told me you were come. How do you find your dear mama?" Without pause, she prattled on, relating all her news—listing the number of times Dr. Laidlaw had called, what he had said, in minute detail, on each successive visit, and how much good Devereux's own visit must now do his poor mama.

Devereux stood up and crossed to the window to curb his mounting irritation. Cousin Amelia was a good soul, devoted to his mother, for whom nothing was too much trouble; it was a pity that she was also a fool!

The catalog wore on: ". . . but she has now found a new friend . . . a dear child! And what do you think, cousin? She is French—such a treat for dear Dominique!"

The duchess saw her son stiffen.

He pivoted slowly. "Madalena?"

"Yes, *mon fils,*" she said quietly. "She has been coming daily these weeks past. We have become very close. You do not mind?"

"Mind—why should I mind?" His mother was offhand, but he wore the shuttered look he had always assumed as a boy when he did not wish one to pry.

"I have no idea," she said innocently. "But Madalena seemed to feel that she must stay away when you are home."

"Silly child! I'll set her straight."

He was descending the staircase as Madalena stepped into the hall. They eyed each other in brooding silence— the duke impassive, Madalena wide-eyed and pale and with a heart hammering so that he must hear it. The dogs came bounding forward from their place beside the hearth, and she bent thankfully to speak with them, just long enough to regain her composure.

"You seem very popular with Castor and Pollux," he observed dryly.

"Yes, we are great friends." She hoped her voice did not betray her agitation as she added with a touch of defiance, "I am visiting your mama."

"So she tells me. I trust you will not be so foolish as to stay away on my account."

"Why ever should I do so?"

"I was under the impression that such was your intention."

"Well, then, I have changed my mind!" She lifted her chin and wondered at the sudden gleam of amusement as his eye traveled from her to the dogs. Casually he leaned forward and retrieved a broken sprig of blossom from her hair.

"And where did you come to this great decision? In the shrubbery?"

A hand flew guiltily to her mouth, and then suddenly, unexpectedly, she began to chuckle. "Oh, but it was quite ridiculous! These silly creatures would not leave, and I was excessively uncomfortable! I prayed that you would not come to look."

He frowned. "I am only sorry that you found it necessary to hide."

"Oh, it was an impulse! You know how I am given"—she broke off on a gasp, and her final words were scarcely audible—"to impulse!" Hot color flared and died; for an instant there was a look of desperate vulnerability, and then she had recovered herself to say in a stifled voice, "Your mama—I must go!"

He made no effort to detain her.

Over the following days the duchess watched Madalena mask her anguish with a brightness that hurt. She tackled her son one evening as he sat with her. His profile was not encouraging; candlelight threw up the high-bossed cheekbones and emphasized the intolerant thrust of jaw. Feeling her eyes upon him, he turned and smiled, and at once her heart swelled with fierce maternal pride. *Dieu!*

How many women were blessed with such a son! If only . . .

"*Chéri,* could you not be less of a bear with Madalena?" The smile vanished abruptly. "You see? Even to mention her makes you cross! Was what she did so dreadful that you cannot be a little kind? She tries so hard . . ."

"Urged on, no doubt, by you."

"It grieves me to know she is unhappy," she said steadily, "and to know that my son is the cause."

"Leave it, Maman! Don't meddle! Madalena is a child. If you don't encourage her, she will recover."

"Will she, my son? And what of you—will you also recover?"

He flung himself out of the chair. The duchess watched his taut, unyielding back with distress. The outstretched hand gripping the chair back showed every vein, every hard-ridged sinew; the words, when they came, seemed torn from him.

"It wouldn't do, Maman—and you know it! I'm not the man for Madalena. Just for a while, back there in London, she almost convinced me that it would work, but—God help me—it was madness even to think it! She is *so* young, so impetuous, so pathetically, *damnably* trusting! And I'm just not worth it!"

The duchess was near to tears. "Devereux—oh, my dearest! You do yourself too much injustice!"

"Do I, Maman?" He came suddenly to kneel at her feet, as he had not done since he was little. "Do I? Be honest." His voice was harsh; the eyes he raised to her were bleak. *"You know what kind of man I am*—and I do not know if I can change. If you had a daughter like Madalena, would you really entrust her to such as I?"

She cupped his face very gently with trembling hands. "I will tell you this, child—you are, in all things, so very like your father, and yet, from the day of our marriage, my Justin never caused me one moment of distress." She saw that he was not convinced. "Oh, well, you must do as you think best. But I beg you, do not go on punishing Madalena as well as yourself."

Chapter 5

MADALENA LAY LISTENING to the clock downstairs chiming the hour—one o'clock. Sleep seemed as far away as ever. It had been a better day, this one—a better week, in fact. Armand, who had been absent on a visit, was home again and had brought his friend Daniel Merchent with him. He was a very personable young man, this Mr. Merchent, and Madalena would have been less than human had she not enjoyed his undoubted admiration.

With Phoebe to make up a four, there had been parties and much laughter. Also, she was able to see Devereux every day, and there was a kind of happiness in having him so near. Almost, she imagined, his manner toward her was softening a little. She sighed and was about to turn over for sleep when there was a sound in the passage.

Pulling on a wrapper, she padded to the door. Armand and Daniel Merchent were creeping toward the stairs, carrying their boots.

"Armand! What are you doing?"

Guiltily they spun around. Her brother flapped an urgent hand. *"Doucement,* child! You will rouse the house!"

"You are dressed for the outside."

"Just a late stroll," murmured Daniel.

"In so furtive a manner—and at such an hour?" She looked from one to the other. "Oh, this I do not believe!"

"It matters little what you believe," snapped Armand. "Go back to your bed."

"Not until I know what it is you do, for it is entirely probable that you will take a chill, and then you will be ill again."

"Tais-toi, imbécile!"

"Imbécile, yourself! I will not be quiet, for you know I speak the truth."

"And I am sick of being pampered! Tante Esmé is worse than Papa! Dr. Laidlaw said plenty of fresh air— and I tell you, I have been many times in the night air at Daniel's without taking a chill!"

"Children . . . children! I beg you!" Daniel soothed them. "Mademoiselle Madalena, it is a pleasant night for walking, and perhaps a little exploring. . . ."

"We have seen a light flashing up near the headland."

Madalena stirred uneasily. "One often sees lights. I think it must be the ships out at sea."

"Or your friend Lytten doing a little . . . trading," suggested Armand wickedly.

Daniel Merchent flashed him a warning glance; he looked annoyed.

So, that was it! Madalena made up her mind at once. "Wait. I shall come with you."

"You will do no such thing!" hissed her brother. "It is no business for girls."

"Bah!" Madalena turned on her heel. As the door clicked shut behind her, she flew to a drawer. Her nightgown slid to the floor, and she began to drag on her breeches. *"Parbleu—c'est infâme!* Not for a girl, indeed!" Impatiently she fastened her shirt and wrestled with the jacket, which had grown uncommonly tight. *Dieu me sauve!* Did she not know more of it than they did, the stupid ones! But what if they ran into Dev? Of a surety, he would be very angry!

Outside, the two young men had vanished, and she went straight to the place where she had encountered

Devereux on that first night and where she had watched him take the track to the beach below Lytten Manor.

It was a very different night, this—warm and still and heavy with the scent of grasses and clover. Clusters of wild primroses carpeted the way, and mingled with it all was the salty tang of the sea. The deep velvet sky was strewn with stars, fading over the sea to a pale turquoise light that was almost as clear as day.

Madalena began to pick her way down the steep path; halfway down, she stopped. There was a noise—like a cry, quickly stifled. She waited, heart drumming, but there was nothing. A sea bird, perhaps. The path began to level out and widen into a flat expanse of grass before the final drop to the beach. Somewhere below her was the jetty where Devereux's yacht was berthed.

She hesitated, and then, ahead of her—no more than a few yards—she saw the outline of a figure bent over something on the ground.

Now, what must she do? It might, of course, be Armand or Daniel. But if it were not? She must inch forward, the better to see. . . .

The blow caught her quite unawares from behind. She was flung to the ground, the breath driven from her body. Gasping, she struggled to rise, and found a boot planted firmly between her shoulders.

"Got the varmint!"

"Bring him here, Jason." Madalena would never have recognized the voice had she not been addressed once before in just such tones. She was hauled unceremoniously to her feet and propelled forward.

Devereux looked down at her, his face a hostile mask in the luminous light from the sea. "Well, Madalena, it seems you did not heed my warnings. That was foolish of you."

Madalena scarcely heeded the cold words; her eyes were fixed on what he held. His glance followed hers to the knife, and without a word he pushed it into his pocket.

She didn't want to look at what was on the ground. Her throat tightened to suffocation, and fear ran like a chill flame along her spine. But she had to know.

The eyes stared sightlessly upward, and the sudden surge of relief that it was not either of the boys turned quickly to horror, for Madalena at once recognized the man. It was the one who had accosted Devereux that day in the park—the one with whom he was so angry. The scarred face was unmistakable.

She felt sick. "He is dead?"

"Quite dead." His voice was grim.

"Armand and Mr. Merchent are somewhere on the cliffs." The words came out in a rush—it was not in the least what she had meant to say. Devereux cursed softly and turned aside to rap out orders to his man Jason, who heaved the body across a broad shoulder and disappeared into the darkness.

"And now, Madalena, what am I to do about you?" It was quietly said, but there was cold fury in every word, in the way he looked. Panic suffocated her. She turned to run, but was seized and held in vicelike fingers. "No. This time you will listen—unless you want to end up like our late friend. I do not play games. *I will not tolerate* any unwarranted meddling—from you, or your brother, or his friends!"

He shook her. "You will never come near these cliffs again at night, do you hear? You will go home now, and you will say nothing. In fact, if you are wise, you will wipe this night's happenings from your mind."

Wild-eyed, she twisted from his grasp, and this time he let her go. She ran, half-stumbling across the turf and up the path, her feet skidding on the loose shale.

Back at the house there was no sign of the others, and Madalena crept up to her room. She flung herself on the bed, hands pressed to her pounding temples; every sense, every nerve end, was screaming denial that Dev could be a murderer, but in a corner of her mind a small cold voice was saying that it must be so.

On the following morning, Madalena was subdued. Armand attributed her silence to pique, and since, incredibly, the two young men appeared to have seen and heard nothing, she confined herself to retorting that she thought their nocturnal jaunt very silly. Daniel Merchent gave her a keen look but said nothing.

When, later, she arrived at Lytten Manor, it was to find that the duke had left at first light.

Madalena plucked nervously at her handkerchief. "Do you know . . . what does Dev *do* when he goes away?"

The duchess examined closely the white face that was all eyes. She chose her words with care. "I do not know, child, and I have always deemed it wiser not to ask. Sometimes, with those we love, it is better just to trust."

"Yes, but suppose . . ." She stopped suddenly, aware how her words might worry her dear friend. "Oh, it is nothing. I am being silly."

She waited and waited, but there came no word of a body being found; doubtless it had been carefully disposed of; the thought made her shudder.

Mr. Merchent had made a most favorable impression on his first visit to Ivy Mount. Such a nice boy, Mrs. Vernon confided to her husband, and so much more suitable! In spite of Lytten's being a duke and having a considerable fortune, one could not but be a little anxious—Madalena was so . . . headstrong. Still, it had all come to naught. She had made it quite clear to Mr. Merchent that he would always be most welcome.

Since the brigadier had seldom lent more than half an ear to anything his wife had said in the ten years since his retirement, he merely grunted and observed that De Brussec might possibly desire some say in the ordering of his daughter's future.

Fortunately, perhaps, Mrs. Vernon's attention was at this moment diverted by the arrival of a letter from John Brownlow's parents, inviting them for a short stay.

Madalena viewed the prospect with mixed feelings; it would be very nice to make such a visit, and of course it was kind of the Brownlows to invite her also, but it meant leaving the duchess, whose health had been the cause of some concern over the past few days.

Dr. Laidlaw had been in attendance morning and evening, and with the reluctant permission of her aunt, who thought it undesirable for a young girl to be cooped up so much with an ailing woman, Madalena had taken to spending a good part of each day at Lytten Manor. She was becoming frightened. Her own mama's last illness was no more than a dim memory, for as children they had been shielded from most of the distress.

But now she must sit for hour upon hour watching her dear friend struggle for breath and grow daily more frail . . . and she no longer believed the platitudes that were handed out to her. Finally, Madalena waylaid the good doctor and demanded without preamble, "Doctor, you will please to tell me how bad is the duchess."

Dr. Laidlaw was a large, comfortable man, a kindly man, and he had taken a fancy to this youngster, and to her brother, whom he had treated once or twice and who was already much improved.

Beneath comical eyebrows, his eyes were compassionate. "Her grace has these attacks from time to time. They are distressing to behold, especially for someone as fond of her as I know you are. But we are doing all we can."

His voice died away under her very straight look.

"*Voyons,* you are telling me only what I already know, monsieur. But me, I am not entirely a fool"—her own voice faltered for a moment, and he saw her gather herself to continue—"and I can see that each attack is worse than the last. I ask myself how long it can continue thus."

Dr. Laidlaw returned her look with eyes grown dark

with the hopeless anguish of one who strives to do all that it is in his power to do, knowing that it is not enough. The duchess had been his patient for many years. He had the greatest admiration for her courage. She radiated a simplicity of joy that only the young in heart possess. Strange that this child should have the same elusive quality.

"Her heart is wearing itself out," he admitted bitterly, "and there is little I can do—save to alleviate her suffering."

"How long does she have?"

He shrugged. "At her present rate of deterioration, perhaps three months, with careful nursing—perhaps less. The human spirit is an unfathomable quantity; I have seen it hold the frailest body alive for an incredible space of time." He saw hope spring into her eyes, and shook his head. "I am sorry, child—even her grace's brave spirit cannot long support a heart that is worn out."

There was complete silence in the room. Madalena held out a hand that trembled slightly and was cold. "*Merci,* monsieur—I thank you for telling me," she said with careful politeness, and his heart ached for her.

When Madalena took her usual chair near the duchess's bed, her embroidery frame lay idle in her lap.

The duchess moved restlessly on the fine lace pillows, and her bright blue eyes, now blurred with drugs, rested thoughtfully on the young face that betrayed so much more than she realized.

"You are . . . very quiet, *ma petite.*"

Madalena jumped. A little color stained her cheeks. "Oh! I am sorry. I thought you wished to sleep. Would you like me to talk . . . or to read for a little?"

"I would like to know . . . what is troubling you."

The girl's head was bent. She jabbed at her sewing. "I was thinking that perhaps I will not go with Tante Esmé and Phoebe, after all."

"Because of me?"

"Oh, no," she cried, overbrightly, "but Phoebe will not need me, you know, when she is to be with her John. . . ."

"Madalena!" Her name was whispered with such feeling, but she rushed heedlessly on, almost choking over the words.

"Of course, it is kind of them to include me, but I should be very much *de trop*."

"Child! Child, you must not mind so much!"

Madalena stared at her, her eyes enormous with tears held back, and her mouth twisted awry. With a sob she dropped to her knees and buried her face in the soft pink counterpane.

"Oh, but I am wicked!" came her muffled wail. "You must have no upset, and be very quiet—and I make a big fool of myself."

Trembling fingers moved in the red-gold curls, soothing, reassuring. "It does not matter, *ma chérie*. It matters only . . . that you are unhappy. And so I think . . . it will be good for you to go away for a little while."

Madalena stirred in protest.

"No, let me finish, child. I know that it is not good that you spend so much time with me, but you see . . . I am too selfish to send you away."

"Oh, no!" This time Madalena did straighten up. "You are the least selfish person I know!"

The duchess was finding concentration difficult, but she was determined to finish. She tapped the tearstained cheek gently.

"You will go with your little cousin—to please me. I will promise to be . . . very good . . . while you are gone, and you will see how much better I am when you return."

Chapter 6

THE SMALL FRENCH cove lay deserted and swathed in mist. The track wound up from the beach to where a squat stone building concealed itself behind a wildly contorted windbreak of tree and scrub, stripped in places to the bareness of bleached bones by the constant onslaught of the prevailing winds.

The house, too, appeared deserted, but his grace the Duke of Lytten ignored it, making his way instead to the stables at the rear, where a tethered gelding whinnied a soft welcome. In a matter of moments he was riding up the track to the road, in his pocket a pass in the name of Philip Mornay, on which was scrawled an unmistakable signature. For a moment he paused to look back. Somewhere in the mist below, Jason waited for the tide. In ten days from now he would return.

One kilometer short of Caudebec the horse cast a shoe. Cursing, Devereux dismounted and led the animal, turning off the road presently to follow a succession of smaller roads, until he stood at last before a pair of high wrought-iron gates beyond which lay a charming little villa.

A groom appeared at once to relieve him of the horse, and then a magnificent black majordomo was ushering him into a purple, gilded salon. Almost at once a vision in deep rose tiffany whisked into the room—petite, blond, and generously endowed with curves.

This was Madame de Marron, a friend of many years' standing, a child bride widowed during the Terror, who had survived the experience by being spirited away to America through the good offices of friends and with most of her husband's fortune intact. There she remained until it was deemed safe to return. She now lived for the most part quietly in the country, but because her sympathies were frankly pro-Bourbon, she had long since decided to make what contribution she could to hastening the downfall of Napoleon Bonaparte and restoring to France her rightful king.

On one of her infrequent visits to Paris, she had sought out Prince Talleyrand, whose path she had crossed on more than one occasion in America. Over a series of intimate little dinners she had made her views known to him, and although he had been ambiguously evasive on the question of the emperor's successor, he had been pleased to make considerable use of her conveniently situated villa as a safe house for his agents.

She tripped across the room now to embrace Devereux. "Janine!" He stood back at last, retaining her hands. "Exquisite as ever, I see!"

"Oh, as to that, *chéri* . . ." She pouted prettily. "You find me practically *en déshabillé!* I was not expecting you."

His gaze became sharply quizzical. "No, my dear. However, it has become imperative that I should visit Paris. Paul Leclerc is dead."

In a few brief words he put her in the picture. "I blame myself in part. He was obsessed with the notion that he was being followed—and I fear I dismissed his wild stories as outbursts of hysteria."

Janine was sympathetic. "He was an odd little man, to be sure, but one could trust him implicitly . . . and that is worth much in these days of plot and counterplot . . . with Talleyrand the most devious of the lot!"

Devereux grimaced. "The old fox will be furious! That is why I thought I had best break the news to him personally. If you can furnish me with a fresh horse . . ."

"Oh, but you will stay for tonight? A few hours can make little difference, after all." She wrinkled her delightful little nose, coaxing, provocative, and all woman—the invitation subtly veiled, but unmistakable. He felt all the old stirring of the blood. He allowed his glance to encompass the tantalizing green eyes, lingering over the softly parted lips and the creamy perfection of her skin. And a picture came unbidden to his mind of a little *gamine* with a too-wide smile.

Deliberately he thrust the thought from him and accepted her invitation, if she would take him in all the dust of his journey.

"This is no problem!" Janine tugged on a bell rope, and almost at once the black servant reappeared.

"Samson, Monsieur Mornay will stay for tonight. Provide him with whatever he may require."

"*Oui,* madame." The voice was cultured, the manner deferential, but not obsequious.

Janine de Marron was much envied for her majordomo. She had first come upon him during her stay in America, in the service of a wealthy New Orleans family, and had been much intrigued by this young slave with the magnificent physique and quiet demeanor, who had been educated by a sympathetic padre. She had prevailed upon the family to sell him, and having given him his freedom, she offered him the position in her household which he had now filled for many years, to their mutual satisfaction, though many had sought to lure him away.

In a luxuriously appointed bedchamber Samson supervised the bringing of warm water and soft towels so that their guest might rid himself of his grime, before assisting him into a shirt of finest lawn, with more lace and ruffles than he was accustomed to wearing.

"I believe this will fit; monsieur's own shirt will be freshly laundered for the morning." By no hint had the majordomo ever betrayed that he knew Devereux's true rank. He said now, "M'sieur has no objection to wearing one of my shirts?"

Devereux looked down and then quizzically at the other's frankly dandified dress. "I doubt I shall do it justice," he murmured.

There was the briefest answering glimmer in the black man's eye, and then a lackey was bringing in Devereux's boots, now buffed to a gleaming perfection, and his coat, freshly sponged and pressed. Samson helped him into the coat, smoothing it almost lovingly across the superb shoulders.

"And now, if monsieur would care to step downstairs, there is a particularly fine claret that we have recently purchased. I would value monsieur's opinion. . . ."

Monsieur's opinion having been duly given in favor of the vintage, he stretched himself out in Janine's most comfortable chair to await her arrival.

Over a dinner tenderly prepared by Janine's Monsieur Choumil, of which the *chef-d'oeuvre* was a *matelote à la bourguignonne* that defied description, they talked freely and with the ease of old friends.

Janine, like Serena Fairfax, understood Devereux, and she had sensed at once the difference in him. Could it be that someone had at last succeeded in piercing the impenetrable fortress of his heart? Yet she sensed also that he was not happy. She knew a momentary stab of jealousy, even of anger. Could it be that this woman did not appreciate her good fortune? That would be ironic indeed, for until now Dev had only to lift his finger!

He would not be drawn out, however, and continually steered the conversation away from his own affairs. They discussed at great length the discontent that was rife in both countries—stemming in France from Bonaparte's ever-growing ambition, which was bleeding the country of both its manpower and its resources. England likewise was suffering; the continuing blockade of Continental ports had now been aggravated by rumors that America would declare war on Britain at any moment. The damage to trade was already bringing disaster to industry and an alarming rise in the price of food.

The assassination of Prime Minister Spencer Perceval in the lobby of the House of Commons on May 11, though the random act of a madman, seemed symptomatic of the general unrest.

Devereux lay back in his chair and contemplated the glowing depths of his wineglass. "You know, my dear Janine, the sooner this war is at an end, the better pleased I shall be."

"Oh, but how is this, *chéri?* Until now, you have relished the challenge afforded you in the work you do."

He smiled faintly. "Perhaps I am growing old."

"Old? You?" Her laugh trilled out. "I think you are in your cups! Listen, and I will tell you something to make you sit up. There has been built a small harbor not many miles from where you come ashore, and there is much smuggling."

Devereux sighed. "There is always smuggling—the navy is powerless to end it. . . ."

"Ah, but this is different, *chéri!* It is not a matter of a few casks of brandy or a little tea or laces for madame. No, I tell you, this is a much bigger enterprise—and more sinister. Important men have been down from Paris, and I have it on fairly reliable authority that consignments are regularly imported—army overcoats, and boots, thousands of pairs of boots, and arms!"

Devereux whistled and sat forward. "You are sure about this?"

"There is a colonel in the National Guard who seems to find me irresistible!" Janine fluttered her eyelashes demurely. "Also, he does not have a strong head for brandy. You would be surprised the things I learn!"

"Then we must ensure that his indiscretions are further turned to good account," said his grace softly.

Paris was still snoring fitfully when Devereux rode in and turned his weary horse toward the poorer quarter of the city. Here the upper stories of the houses leaned drunkenly over the narrow streets. In a few hours these squalid, cobbled ways would be jammed by a strident melee of men, horses, and wagons that would send the less fortunate scrambling for their lives, but for now there was only the flotsam of the previous night—an occasional prone body huddled for comfort against a wall, and the garbage that drifted sluggishly as a capricious morning breeze began to roll back the clouds of night.

The concierge poked a bleary head out of his cubbyhole as Devereux climbed wearily to the room on the second floor that was his *pied-à-terre* when in Paris, and on recognizing Monsieur Mornay, muttered a brusque greeting and withdrew.

After a few hours' sleep, Devereux emerged again into one of the quieter back streets, refreshed and resplendent in a fine mulberry coat, buff pantaloons, and gleaming black hessians. His steps led him unerringly in the direction of a small *patisserie,* lured by the fragrant smell of fresh baking. He ducked automatically beneath the lintel as he pushed open the door to the insistent jangling of bells.

An enormously fat woman waddled through from the back of the shop, grumbling and wiping flour from her hands as she came. She threw up her hands at the sight of him, and her ample bosom heaved beneath the all-enveloping apron; a chuckle began way down and gradually erupted, until all her chins were quivering and the bright button eyes disappeared in a mass of creases.

"Monsieur, you have come back to us at last! Come in, come in! Ah, I know why you are here—heh?" She wagged a playful finger as she propelled him before her into the back room. "You hope for some of Mama Bertha's lobster patties. You have not broken your fast? Then you are just in time, *bien sûr!*"

Under his nose the table was spread with a snowy cloth

and the steaming patties placed before him, together with
a cold truffled capon. From a cupboard she triumphantly
produced a bottle. "See? I remember your likes—and for
you, I keep always a small supply."

Devereux had been patronizing Madame Bertha regularly over the ten years since he had first acquired the
room in the Rue Blanc. She had taken the fascinating and
slightly mysterious Monsieur Mornay at once under her
wing. On one occasion she had ventured surprise that so
virile a young man was not taken for the army, and had
received for answer so significant a look that her affection
thereafter had become tinged with awe.

As he did full justice to the patties, he quizzed her as to
the mood of Paris.

It was not good, she told him with a heavy sigh, and began to knead her dough with a fine fury.

"It is not so much that money is short—or food, for
that matter; the people do not starve. But neither do they
laugh anymore. For more than twenty years, it seems, we
have been a country at war, and mothers have waited with
hopeless eyes for the sons who will never return . . .
wives struggle to support their demanding families un-
aided, or with menfolk helplessly crippled."

Madame Bertha brandished her rolling pin. "And for
what, *mon fils?* Heh? You tell Mama Bertha—are we any
the better for it all? I tell you that in the beginning the emperor gave us back our pride—and that was fine! But now,
the army goes to seek greater triumphs—and maybe disaster—and we womenfolk see only that the Flowers of
France perish so that one man may pursue his dream of
conquest! No, *mon fils,* if some of us now wish the emperor dead—who is to blame us?"

It was a long speech. She blew noisily into her handkerchief and glared at Devereux, bright-eyed. "And there is a
fine treasonable statement for you, if you like!"

He stood up from the table and laid a comforting arm

about the shaking shoulders. "Courage, Mama Bertha, you will have your peace yet."

The sun was high when Devereux reached the luxurious mansion on the Rue Saint Florentin. A small town carriage was just leaving, and he caught a brief glimpse of bright curls beneath a charming chip bonnet.

He was shown into a lavishly appointed library, where he was presently joined by a slight, pallid-faced man of middle years, elegant to the point of dandyism, who leaned heavily on a jeweled malacca cane. This was Charles Maurice de Talleyrand-Périgord, Prince de Bénevént—ex-bishop of Auton—and, without a doubt, the most dissolute, the wiliest, the most astute and devious man in all of France.

He had kept his head through the Revolution, and after a prudent sojourn in America had returned during the difficult days of the Directory, surviving unpopularity to make himself indispensable to the young Bonaparte, and thereafter, to tread a dangerous path of intrigue, corresponding constantly with numerous heads of state, both friend and foe, under the very nose of his emperor.

He now extended a graceful, beruffled hand in welcome. He indicated a comfortable chair near the window and lowered himself slowly into the one opposite. An unfortunate accident in early childhood, when a nurse had dropped him from a dresser, had left him with an irremediable lameness, so that he was unable to stand for any length of time without great fatigue.

"I had not expected to see you, duke," he said in his thin voice. "I trust that all is well?"

Devereux explained the nature of his visit and caught a fleeting glimpse of annoyance in the cold, almost fishlike eyes before the heavy eyelids came down to obscure all expression. There was silence in the room while the prince's subtle brain digested the news and its implications.

"It is unfortunate," he said at last. "I do not believe I

can replace Leclerc at the present time." The cold, piercing eyes looked full into Devereux's. "Would you, Monseigneur le duc, be willing to assume his role—temporarily?"

Devereux was taken aback. "Would that be wise, highness?"

Talleyrand shrugged his elegantly clad shoulders. "Who can say what is wise? It is essential that I have someone I can trust. Events are fast approaching which will be difficult . . ."

"I was speaking with the Russian ambassador before I left London. He was amazingly confident that Napoleon will come to grief in the great trackless wastes of his country—that he will be lured farther and farther from his supply bases until he is decimated by the winter."

"He would not be told." Almost, Talleyrand smiled. "Yes, I do believe our 'little man' is at last overreaching himself! We must be ready for the consequences."

With an apparent change of subject, Devereux said casually, "I was not aware that Aimée de Coigny was known to your highness. I was not mistaken in seeing her leave as I arrived?"

The bland expression never altered. "Ah, yes, Madame de Coigny! An impetuous young woman. She is endeavoring to win me over to the Bourbon cause, you know." A small, malicious smile touched the ironic mouth. "It does no harm to let her run on."

"And is there any case for Louis XVIII, do you think?"

"Who knows, my friend? The emperor's power is slipping. His day as a force against the revolution is long gone. It is all very well that he destroys equality, but we must still have liberty. We need laws. With him it is impossible." The voice had grown harsh. He stopped and then resumed obliquely, "I may count on you, then, may I not? Had Leclerc lived, I believe I should still have called upon you. One does not treat through the Aimée de Coignys of this world."

There was little Devereux could do but assent. He rose to leave. "Tell me, highness—are you acquainted with Etienne de Brussec?"

The hooded eyes widened a little. "I know Monsieur de Brussec, of course—a most popular man with the common people, though he does not count me among his friends." Again the elegant shoulders moved, and he smiled thinly. "It seems he does not altogether trust me! Our worthy lawyer is that most dangerous and foolhardy of creatures— a completely honest man! I fear it may yet be his undoing."

"So I am led to believe. Can you perhaps give me his address?"

Devereux sensed a certain reluctance and said hastily, "Do not alarm yourself, highness. My business with De Brussec is of a purely personal nature. His children, as you may know, are in England with their aunt."

"Quite so. Twins, are they not? And one of them a rather captivating girl child, as I remember." For an instant the cold eyes gleamed, before resuming their habitual enigmatic expression.

"He lives out at Plassy—safe from the corrupting influences of the city. I will write his address for you." Talleyrand grasped the malacca cane and came painfully to his feet. "Be careful, duke! I have much influence, it is true, but if Demarest's secret police arrest you, there is little even I can do! And one thing more, duke—if you are in a position to do so, advise our worthy friend to caution. France can ill afford to lose such a man!"

His business in Paris completed, Devereux made good time back to the coast. Finding himself with some hours to kill before Jason could be expected, and being strangely reluctant to revisit Janine, he resolved to discover for himself the site of this supposed concealed harbor. If it indeed existed, and if he could pinpoint the spot with some degree of accuracy, it would make the navy's job that much easier.

He urged the tired gelding along a narrow track parallel

with the cliffs and presently came to a place where an even rougher track meandered down toward the beach between high banks. He dismounted and tethered the horse before moving cautiously forward until he could see below. Half-way down, a ramshackle inn clung to the cliff face, and below that was a small quayside bustling with activity.

He had just determined to take a closer look when a soft nicker from the horse and a highly developed sixth sense alerted him. He spun around; a pistol ball smacked into the ground where he had been, and a second scorched his sleeve. There were two men advancing on him with knives, and with no time to draw and aim his own pistol, he reached instead for the sword bayonet that he had wrested from the hand of a dead rifleman at Badajos in order to defend himself and had found so useful a weapon that he had kept it thereafter.

The next few minutes were spent fending off a particularly vicious assault, made the more unnerving by the total silence in which it was conducted, broken only by the hiss of heavy breathing. As the two men came at him in a concerted attack, Devereux shot out his foot and brought the nearer one crashing to the ground. This gave him vital seconds in which to dispose of his accomplice, who came on at him with renewed ferocity. It was his undoing, for at the last moment Devereux feinted and brought his blade up, spitting the man with deadly accuracy.

He struggled to free the blade, aware that the second man was on his feet again. But it had jammed. He wrenched desperately at it, cursing its awkwardness, a cold sweat running down his back. When all seemed lost, a shot rang out, and the second man staggered and fell.

Devereux straightened, breathing hard, to see the elegant, imperturbable figure of Samson astride a pure white mare, a smoking horse pistol protruding incongruously from the heavy lace ruffles at his wrist.

"My thanks!" he gasped. "I don't know how the devil you come to be here, but . . ."

"I was returning from performing some small commissions for madame." The big man pushed the pistol back into its holster and swung from the saddle. "I saw you ahead of me on the road—and this *canaille* also. When you turned onto the cliff path and they followed, I took it upon myself to do likewise."

"As well for me that you did, man—I believe I owe you my life."

The majordomo permitted himself a slight smile. "I doubt it would have come to that, monsieur—but I am happy to have been of service."

Devereux stirred one of the bodies with the toe of his boot, rolling him onto his back. "Do you recognize either of them?"

"No, monsieur, but they are not common brigands, I think. Observe the dress."

Methodically they went through the pockets of both men, and straightened up at last with a neat pile of notebooks and documents. Their eyes met.

"Not much doubt as to who they are," Devereux said curtly.

"Secret police."

"So. What do we do with them? Before long, someone will undoubtedly come looking."

Samson returned him a bland look. "If monsieur will assist me in getting them across the mare's back, I will engage to dispose of their bodies where they will never be found."

Devereux grinned suddenly. "I begin to see why Madame de Marron values you so highly. You are obviously a man of many parts."

The job done, Samson took up the reins. "I think you should go, monsieur, if you would not miss the tide." He inclined his head courteously. "I wish you an uneventful crossing."

Devereux picked up his hat, which had come off in the fight, and swung into the saddle. He stretched down a hand to the black man, who was unprepared for such a gesture. A strange expression crossed his face; slowly he extended his hand and found it firmly gripped.

Devereux said warmly, "My thanks again, Samson!"

For the first time, Samson betrayed his knowledge of Devereux's true rank. There was a moistness in his eyes as he replied huskily, "No, Monseigneur le duc, it is for me to thank you!"

Chapter 7

MADALENA WAS LATE. When young Tom, the footman, opened the door to her, she rushed past him impetuously up the staircase without listening to what he was saying. The poor duchess would be wondering whatever had become of her, but Phoebe had been most insistent that she decide upon the patterns for the dresses she was to take with her into Wiltshire.

Entering the bedchamber, she was astonished to see so eager a light in her dear friend's eye. Then her heart gave a great lurch, and she leaned weakly against the door. From a chair beside the bed a figure unfolded itself—a figure clad informally in shirt and breeches, with a crimson cravat knotted casually at the neck, whose glance encompassed her in so strange, so enigmatic a fashion that, when she thought of their last encounter, the blood came and went in her face.

The duchess beckoned her forward eagerly, and Madalena bent to kiss the now painfully thin cheek. "Come, *ma chérie,* I have something for you!" She indicated a package beside her on the bed.

Madalena looked from mother to son and back again before tearing away the wrappings. She stood very still, staring down at what lay revealed.

"Is it as it should be, child?"

Madalena touched the little alabaster figure of the kneeling Madonna with tentative fingers, quite unable to speak.

"I described it to Devereux as you described it to me," continued the duchess. "I think he has been most clever to discover one so soon."

Madalena's eyes were blurred. She swallowed on the enormous lump in her throat. "It is *incroyable!*" she whispered, sinking into the chair and lifting the little statue with reverence onto her knee.

Devereux watched the totally absorbed expression on her face with a sense of satisfaction. He leaned toward his mother, and their eyes met in a look of complete understanding. He dropped a light kiss on her forehead.

"*À bientôt, chérie.* I must go."

Madalena looked up then, frowning. "Oh, but you do not leave your mama again—so soon?"

His satanic brows twitched. "I fear I must—but for a few days only, so pray remove that look of disapproval."

She turned her attention back to the little figure, marveling at its exact resemblance to her own. Absently, her thumb strayed in an old familiar gesture, smoothing, sliding along the narrow plinth, and underneath . . . Her thumb stopped and moved slowly back. Her heart began to thump as she turned the statue over. And then she was standing it carefully on the table and running to the door, leaving behind a very bewildered duchess.

The duke had already reached the bottom of the staircase as she sped after him in a flurry of muslin skirts. She called, and he turned. Two steps above him, she stopped, breathless, her whole body tense.

"Dev? Oh, please . . . I must speak with you!"

He eyed her for a moment in silence and then put out a hand to draw her down the remaining stairs and into the library.

Almost before the door was shut, Madalena blurted out, "The little statue—how did you come by it?"

He considered her quietly. "Why do you ask?"

"Because it is mine." She thought he would deny it, and rushed on without pause, her voice shaking very slightly. "There is no mistake, I promise you! My initials are on the base—where I carved them many years ago."

Devereux wore his stranger's face—severe, withdrawn. It frightened her. And then the hard, brilliant eyes softened into self-mockery. "I never thought of that!" he murmured.

"You knew . . . that it was mine?" Madalena stared. A whole flood of possibilities suddenly unleashed themselves. But through her confusion, one thought superseded all others. "But then"—it was an awed whisper—"but then . . . you must have been in France . . . at Plassy! You must have seen Papa!"

For answer he walked to a Buhl desk on the far wall beside the fireplace. From his pocket he extracted a small gilt key, with which he unlocked one of the drawers. He turned with a letter in his hand.

"You were to have received this anonymously, but there now seems little point."

She sat curled up in an armchair near the window, and Devereux watched the animation in her face as she avidly digested every word, tears rolling silently down her cheeks, to be impatiently brushed aside.

He turned abruptly to the window in the grip of what was for him a new emotion—jealousy! A wild, irrational jealousy that any man, albeit her father, could arouse in her such depths of feeling!

She came at last just to touch his arm. "Thank you," she said simply, and then, half-hesitating: "He is well— Papa?"

"Yes."

"And . . . he is being careful?"

Devereux looked down at her, knowing he could not fob her off with platitudes. "You know your father," he said gravely.

"Oh, yes!" Madalena heaved a great sigh. "Complete integrity can be a very tiresome virtue, but one would not wish him different." She glanced again at the letter. "It is addressed to both of us. You do not think Armand will mind that I have opened it?"

"I doubt it will worry Armand."

"No—and besides, he is away somewhere with Daniel Merchent. He would never expect me to await his return."

"Young Armand is spending a lot of time with Dan Merchent."

She shrugged. "Ah, well, life is a little dull for him here." She grinned impishly. "Kit is so often in town, and to be in a house full of women is tiresome."

"I would rather Armand knew nothing of this," Devereux said abruptly.

"You mean, I should not let him see the letter?"

"No—that is not what I mean. I should simply prefer him to know nothing of my part in its delivery."

Madalena's eyes were troubled, and there was a queer, hollow feeling in the pit of her stomach. "Dev!" she whispered. "What *is* it that you do?"

"No questions, Madalena," he said curtly. "Will you just do as I ask?"

"But of course," she said simply, while the fear crawled insidiously up her spine. "If that is what you wish. I will leave the little statue here also, so that there will be no danger of Armand seeing it."

"Thank you, little one." He took possession of her hands and studied them before carrying first one and then the other to his lips. "I must go. When I return, perhaps we can ride together."

"Oh!" Madalena's voice felt very strange, for her heart

was beating right up in her throat. "I am to go away myself in two days' time with Tante Esmé and Phoebe—to the home of Phoebe's affianced husband." And I very much wish that I were not, she almost added, but since Dev did not appear to feel any great degree of disappointment, she kept silent, and for the remainder of her visit, the duchess found her strangely subdued.

The day for their journey into Wiltshire dawned hot and sultry, so that, before they had covered half the distance, Mrs. Vernon was wilting. She complained bitterly and at great length about everything from the weather to the post boys, and the frustrations of traveling without the support of a man, for it was obvious for all to see that they had been fobbed off with a shockingly winded team at the last change.

The Brownlows' house lay just beyond the little market town of Craigford, which necessitated their traveling the length of the main thoroughfare. Mrs. Vernon wakened from an uneasy doze to behold Madalena leaning suicidally from the window and in a state of great agitation imploring the driver to halt the chaise! *Tout de suite!*

Already nervous of foreigners, and persuaded that it must be a matter of life or death, the post boy complied with a suddenness that all but catapulted the three ladies to the floor.

Deaf to querulous demands that she should explain her extraordinary behavior at once, Madalena continued to hang from the window of the chaise in a manner that caused her aunt to turn pale and almost brought on one of her spasms.

"Child!" she entreated faintly. "I implore you! Only consider what people must think! Consider Phoebe's reputation, if you have no regard for your own!"

But Madalena only presented a shining face to her aunt. "It is Paul Renault! We grew up together at Plassy. I do not at all understand how he is here, but . . ." In the midst of these confused explanations she turned back and waved frantically. "Paul . . . oh, Paul, *mon cher ami . . . viens ici! À moi!*"

The young man so addressed stopped dead in the act of crossing the street. He was a slight, fair young man in a blue uniform coat with red facings. He turned in amazed disbelief on hearing his name so familiarly called.

"Little Maddie!" He gripped his friend's arm convulsively. "Gaston, my friend—do you see? In the chaise—it is Madalena de Brussec! Oh, I do not believe . . ."

In a few strides he was at the door of the chaise, reaching up hands in affectionate greeting to the dear playmate of his childhood.

As they laughed and exclaimed over each other, Mrs. Vernon lay back, inert, convinced that the whole town must by now be witness to the whole deplorable spectacle; her poor Phoebe would never in the future be able to hold up her head among them.

Phoebe herself, while sensible of her mother's feelings, was nonetheless infected by some of Madalena's excitement. She leaned forward eagerly, to find herself looking straight down into a pair of cynically appraising gray eyes. She caught her breath on a startled gasp and withdrew at once in rosy confusion.

Captain Gaston Marceau wondered fleetingly who was the little mouse in the chaise. He shrugged and returned his attention once more to the animated couple at his side.

"But how is it that you are here?" Madalena was demanding. "I do not understand."

"Little goose! This is a parole town. Did you not know? And how are you here, might I ask?"

They exchanged news. Madalena was able to give Paul an account of his family and regretted volubly that Armand was not with her. Paul recounted his adventures leading up to his capture. He would say little of his early imprisonment in the hulks, merely remarking that they were now very tolerably comfortable. There were some two hundred men, he told her, most of them in a converted barracks on the outskirts of the town. A few of the more fortunate officers, including Gaston and himself, however, had been given their parole and were lodging in the town itself.

Madalena at last recollected herself, and hasty introductions were performed. Mrs. Vernon roused a little on learning that the two men were frequent visitors at the Brownlows', and indeed were promised there on the following evening for dinner prior to attending a ball in the local assembly rooms—a piece of information that caused Phoebe's heart to give a treacherous flutter.

Indeed, when the two girls were dressing on the following evening, and Phoebe turned the conversation yet again to the subject of the two Frenchmen, Madalena began to be a little dismayed.

"Phoebe, *chérie,* I beg you, do not let Captain Marceau lead you to be . . . indiscreet!"

Phoebe bridled and flounced across to sit at the dressing mirror. The new blue lutestring dress was one of several made especially for this visit. Surely it made her eyes seem twice as bright. "I am sure I don't know what you mean," she countered evasively.

"Yes you do," said Madalena flatly. "He will make you very unhappy if you allow him to do so."

"I don't know how you can say such a thing! You don't even know him."

"I do not need to know him. I know his kind. He is of a hardness, that one. He would amuse himself with you for as long as it pleased him to do so, and then he would walk away without a qualm and leave your heart in little pieces."

Phoebe rounded on her in anger. "Well, I must say that's rich, coming from you! And you still hankering after Lytten in spite of his abominable behavior!"

Raw anguish flared in Madalena's eyes; her face grew as white as her dress, but Phoebe was too incensed to notice. "For me it is different," she said a little unsteadily, "but you have your nice John to consider."

"Oh, he is so dull and unromantic."

"You have never thought so until now." Madalena came and wound her arms around the other girl's unyielding shoulders. "He is right for you, my Phoebe. He is good and kind, and so very British!" In the mirror, her riot of red-gold curls contrasted startlingly with Phoebe's delicate fairness; and her eyes, deeply amber, were urgent in their appeal. "Please believe me. I am right, I promise you."

Phoebe shrugged off her cousin's embrace and sprang up, smoothing the blue dress with impatient fingers. "Goodness! I'm sure I don't know what all the fuss is about. I dare swear Captain Marceau will scarcely notice me."

But later in the evening, as Madalena danced a cotillion with John Brownlow, she was only too aware of Phoebe being partnered by the captain and being treated to that irresistible blend of careless charm and arrogant self-mockery. And Phoebe was responding with eyes that shone like jewels. It was impossible that John Brownlow should not also be aware of his fiancée's complete absorption.

When the captain led Phoebe back to her chair and leaned forward, all attention, Madalena seized John by the hand and propelled him toward the engrossed couple.

The next few minutes were charged with unspoken emotion as general politenesses were exchanged. John was grim and monosyllabic, Phoebe truculent, and the bold captain faintly amused. Only Madalena kept up a nonstop flow of pleasantries, until the music began again, when she gently propelled the reluctant lovers toward the dance floor.

Gaston Marceau leaned a slim shoulder against the wall and folded his arms, watching the proceedings with amused indifference.

"Playing propriety, mademoiselle? Strange—I should not have thought you the type."

"Captain Marceau," Madalena rebuked him severely, "my little cousin is betrothed to Mr. Brownlow, as I think

you well know. I will not have her future put in jeopardy
and her whole life made miserable by such a one as you!"

"*Eh bien?* And what of my misery, mademoiselle—do
you not consider that?"

Madalena's eyes twinkled suddenly. "Not one whit,
monsieur, for I do not believe you are in the least miserable. You are simply consumed with *ennui!*"

The cynicism was back, etched deep in the lines of his
face. "Being a prisoner of war is a boring business!"

She nodded. "Yes, this I can understand. But it does
not excuse your behavior. Phoebe is not fair game for you,
mon capitaine." She gave him a frank, thoughtful look.
"Surely, even here in Craigford, there are those who would
be only too willing to . . . comfort you?"

To her astonishment, Gaston Marceau put back his
head and laughed—and at once he appeared years
younger. "Mademoiselle Madalena, I thank you for re-
minding me how straightforward and practical is the mind
of the Frenchwoman!"

He held out his hands to her. "And now, before young
Paul claims you for yet more of his ennervating childhood
reminiscences, perhaps you will dance with me?"

"But of course, Captain Marceau. And you will please
to flirt no more with Phoebe." Madalena flashed him a wide
grin. "You may flirt just a little with me instead!"

Chapter 8

ARMAND DE BRUSSEC LEANED an arm along the back of
the settle and stared moodily out at the gray sea. A sudden

squall of rain splattered the window, beneath which an ancient inn sign squeaked monotonously back and forth in a stiff breeze.

From the room behind him came the spasmodic murmur of voices interspersed with much high-pitched giggling—a sure sign that Sir Vyvian Courtney was enjoying himself.

Smuggling had offered excitement and romance to the soul of the young Frenchman bored with life in a strange country; waiting with Daniel for Captain Wilkins' schooner to anchor off the Kent coast, avoiding the revenue men, and once even a squadron of dragoons, in order to get the contraband ashore—all this greatly appealed to a young man until recently considered too delicate to attempt the least exertion.

And when Daniel had suggested actually crossing to France with Captain Wilkins, the possibility had filled him with a sudden homesickness that had made him say yes at once, without considering the dangers. Madalena would be away with Tante Esmé—she need never know!

But in his imagination he had not equated a visit to his homeland with being incarcerated in this squalid, uncomfortable inn while Daniel concluded what he termed the boring details of their transactions.

Reexamining the small, busy wharf, Armand estimated that there must be upward of a dozen vessels, everything from trim little ketches and luggers to Captain Wilkins' swift, two-masted schooner—and all, without a doubt, plying the same illicit trade.

The more he thought, the more it seemed inconceivable that such a harbor could exist without someone in authority knowing of it—and thereby sanctioning it! *Mon Dieu!* The thought raised a whole new flood of possibilities!

For example, the man who was now deep in conversation with Daniel—a tall man, stern of countenance, and of a military bearing—of a surety he was no ordinary smuggler. Even as Armand watched, the man gestured toward a pile of crates lying on the wharf, and after further brief discussion, a package changed hands.

Here Armand's thoughts were interrupted. A pair of soft white arms wound themselves seductively around his neck.

"The young monsieur is looking pensive. Babette will remove that frown, heh?"

He stiffened with embarrassment and endeavored to draw away from the full-blown blond. Her cheap perfume nauseated him and made him stumble hoarsely over his words. "No, thank you, mademoiselle."

His politeness enchanted her, sending her at once into peals of laughter; it shook her fast-developing double chins and creased the young face already raddled by paint.

"Did you hear, Jeannette? What a little gentleman! Like I was his sister, if you please!"

The unfortunate comparison with Madalena only aroused further disgust in Armand, but the doxy, undeterred, was already undoing the buttons of his shirt and waistcoat. She slid her hand provocatively inside, where it lay warm against his skin.

"You don't have to be so formal with Babette, *chéri*. Come, I will show you!"

Her breath was offensive so close to his face. Armand clambered to his feet in a panic, almost overturning the settle and sending the girl staggering.

Enraged, she planted herself before him, hands spread aggressively on ample hips, her breasts, already inadequately confined, threatening to burst free at any moment.

"*Sacré Nom!* But you insult me, monsieur!" she spat at him.

Armand, still scarlet with embarrassment, stammered incoherent apologies. He carefully averted his gaze from the sofa, where Vyv was cavorting with the girl's companion.

"Stop it, m'boy!" Vyv's slurred, amused tones were muffled in the doxy's tumbled flounces. "Ye're a damned

dull dog for a froggie! You should learn to take your plea-
sures with more insouciance, more *joie de vivre!*"

There was the unmistakable sound of a playful slap on
bare flesh, followed by shrieks from the girl and much
suggestive whispering.

Babette, incensed at being denied the opportunity to dis-
port herself in similar fashion, poured a further stream of
invective upon them all and slammed from the room, setting every piece of cheap china upon the shabby dresser
rattling.

Armand turned blindly back to the window, swallowing
down his intense revulsion and wishing with all his heart
that he had never become so involved.

The severe-looking man had gone, and Daniel was walking back up the quay toward the inn. A second man came
from the shadows to accost him. He talked rapidly for
some minutes, violent gestures emphasizing the urgency
of his message. Daniel listened with lowered head and then
spoke several sharp words, after which the man scurried
away.

Dan stood for a moment, wrapped in thought, and then
he turned back and went aboard the schooner.

When he finally stepped into the parlor of the inn, he
found Armand sullenly silent and Sir Vyvian blandly setting his clothes to rights. Of the girls there was no sign,
beyond a lingering trace of stale perfume.

"Well, you're a right merry pair, to be sure!" he mused
with a touch of humor. "How would you fancy a spot of
action to liven you up?"

The young nobleman yawned and declared himself
game, but Armand only frowned.

"Action? What is this action you speak of?"

Daniel Merchent walked to the table and poured himself a glass of wine, throwing the young man a long, considering look. "I don't pretend to know what's been going
on here, but if you'll come out of your sulks, boy, I'll give
you my news."

Armand flushed and bit his lip. Dan settled himself on the edge of the table, one booted foot swinging gently back and forth. He sipped his drink, his eyes intent over the rim of the glass.

"You behold in me, my friends, the recipient of a most interesting item of news. There is, as I am reliably informed, a cache of the finest brandy—at least three dozen casks—stored but a few miles up this coast. It is ours for the taking, and Captain Wilkins assures me we have ample room for it."

Sir Vyvian sat forward, brightening visibly. "Dan, dear boy, you behold me all attention! Tell me, do the owners of this brandy give it up willingly—or do we use a little persuasion?"

Dan grinned. "I doubt it will be offered gratuitously, but I believe there is no more than a token guard."

Armand looked from one to the other. "I do not understand what are your intentions. Are we to do some kind of deal for this brandy?"

Vyv slapped his thigh and threw back his head. "I don't believe it, Dan. D'ye know, the lad's a positive innocent!" He rested an amused, kindly eye upon Armand. "Aye, m'boy—you might call it a deal, in a manner of speaking!"

"Oh."

Dan continued smoothly, "There is a reasonably negotiable track along the coast, so I have arranged for horses to be provided. Captain Wilkins will complete his business here and then proceed to that particular stretch of coast, where he will lie to until he receives our signal. He will then dispatch a couple of boats ashore to take us and the brandy on board."

When, after many hours of riding, they were in sight of their objective, the last of the daylight was fading and Armand drew his collar more tightly about his neck against the chill little wind that whipped in off the sea, but his shivering was not entirely due to the cold.

They had a longer wait than they had expected before an answering light flashed from the sea. They turned the horses down toward the beach, and presently, above the slap of waves on shingle, the creaking of oars could be heard, and against the pale outline of the horizon Armand was able to distinguish several figures running up the beach.

The party met where the distorted windbreak of trees bent over the same deserted building that Devereux had previously visited.

The horses were tethered to a stunted bush beside the track, and they made their way in silence to the rear of the building. Armand's unease grew with every step. He caught at Daniel's arm with sudden urgency.

"Why do we proceed with such stealth? I insist that you tell me—are we to steal this brandy?"

Daniel silenced him impatiently. "Well, of course we are to steal it! How else are we to lay our hands on it?"

"But . . . to steal!" Unbidden, his father's face came before him, but Dan swung around on him in sudden anger, and his voice, though hardly above a breath, lashed him.

"A brigands' horde, lad! Fair game for anyone who cares to go after it. Now, stop being squeamish, and for God's sake keep quiet and keep your head down."

They reached the stables where the casks were stacked. The lone occupant of the stable whinnied nervously in his stall, and suddenly the silence erupted into violent pandemonium.

Four men came at them out of the shadows, and amidst the confusion of musket and pistol shots, Dan yelled at the cowering ship's crew to get the barrels shifted. One of the brigands was already dead, spilling out his brains at Dan's feet, but the other three were closing in with vicious-looking knives, and for Armand the next few minutes were blurred with horror.

He was out of his depth, and he knew it. Fear ran through him, freezing his skull; his sleeve was slashed, and a warm spurt of blood trickled down his arm. He fought on in despair, knowing that the end must be inevitable; bad teeth leered above him in a wicked grin, and then the grin became transfixed and a look of disbelief widened the eyes. The man slid to the floor, and Vyv was pulling a knife from his back.

"Merci, mon ami!" gasped Armand. He staggered and wiped the sweat from his face with a shaking hand.

Sir Vyvian grinned at him. "Think nothing of it, dear boy. But I believe we should do something about that arm—you're bleeding like a plaguey stuck pig!"

Sir Vyvian produced from his pocket a large spotted silk handkerchief with which he bound up the gash, tying the final knots with the same panache that he accorded his cravats.

Now that there was time to look about him, Armand saw that the remaining two men had been overcome and lay bleeding and groaning upon the ground.

He turned away abruptly, to lean against the side of the building, fighting sudden nausea. Two seamen scurried past him carrying the last of the brandy casks. Gradually he became aware of raised voices. Dan and Sir Vyvian were engaged in a heated argument.

Dan's voice rose harshly. "There *is* no alternative, damn you! We can't afford to leave witnesses—and you know it!"

He was standing over the two brigands, reloading his pistols.

"No!" The hoarse, involuntary cry was wrung from Armand, and both men raised their heads in surprise, as though they had forgotten his existence. "No!" he pleaded again through chattering teeth. "They are at your mercy. You cannot take their lives in cold blood!"

"Get him down to the boat, Vyv." Daniel's voice was curt, his glance contemptuous.

Sir Vyvian shrugged and took Armand's good arm, urging the protesting boy toward the beach. "Leave it be,

dear old fellow!" he murmured placatingly. "I daresay
Dan is in the right of it—he usually is."

"But . . . God in heaven! One does not kill helpless
men!" Armand reiterated in dazed disbelief. Two shots
rang out, and he shuddered.

Later he lay inert in the cabin, as the schooner turned
for home, averting his gaze as Daniel came clattering down
the companionway.

"I want words with you, boy!" he snapped.

"Of what use are words? They cannot justify—"

"You mistake me. I don't have to justify anything to
you—least of all the deaths of those accursed brigands!"

"They were men!" Armand cried hotly. "Men, injured
and helpless, and you killed them!"

"They were savages, boy. Shall I spell out for you what
would have happened if matters had gone against us? In a
merciful mood they might have slit our throats, but they
are not noted for their mercy! There is a name for them
in these parts—*chauffeurs*." Armand turned his head
away abruptly, his face ashen beneath the red hair.

Daniel's voice continued remorselessly. "It is a kind of
sport with them to roast people alive, so don't waste your
pity on that scum!"

"And are we so much better?" Armand raised himself
painfully on his sound arm. "For it seems to me, my friend,
that we are not the simple smugglers you encouraged me
to believe."

Daniel came to lean over the bunk; gone was the devil-
may-care young Englishman with the laughing eyes. Now
there was menace in every taut line of his body.

"Now, that is what I wanted to speak about," he said
very softly. "Perhaps you have aired your views elsewhere,
my friend. Have you?"

The last two words were rapped out so suddenly that
the boy flinched.

"No! Who would I—?"

"How should I know? Your sister, perhaps?"

"Madalena! But that is absurd. No, I do not discuss what I do with anyone!" cried Armand.

Daniel's eyes were flint-hard. "That had better be the truth, lad, because if I find out who betrayed me . . ."

"I do not understand. What is this talk of betrayal?"

The older man's fist clenched rigidly on the bunk. "Do you know why Wilkins was late keeping the rendezvous? No? Then I will tell you why. Because soon after we left, three frigates of the British Navy sailed in and bombarded the harbor—sank several of my best craft and reduced the quayside to a rubble! Wilkins only got away by the skin of his teeth in the growing darkness."

Armand's face was a study of bewilderment. "Your craft? But I do not understand!"

"It is not necessary for you to understand; suffice it to say that my operations are planned and executed with the utmost care. So how came the British Navy to hear of them? I do not believe in coincidence."

There was no answer.

"Well, I shall find out—make no mistake!" Daniel Merchent's words were low and vehement. "Last night's work has cost me dear, and I must now find a new place to trade."

Armand's bewilderment was slowly turning to horror. "But . . . you are English!"

"Correction, my dear Armand—I was born in England, and my mother was English, but my father was French. He fled to England with my mother at the outbreak of the Terror. And how did England receive my father? I will tell you. My mother's family tolerated him only for her sake, and when he was so unwise as to antagonize someone of importance in the government, they raised not a finger to prevent his being extradited to France, on the flimsiest of evidence, where he was promptly guillotined. A charming tale, is it not?" His tone was scathing.

"I am sorry," Armand muttered inadequately.

"Don't be!" snapped Daniel. "I stopped feeling sorry for

myself a long time ago when my mama died of grief and I learned why. I tell you all this only that you may understand why I feel no degree of loyalty toward either country. This war means only one thing to me—profit! Huge, untapped sources of profit! You have no idea to what lengths some people will go in order to secure what they want . . ."

He stopped suddenly, as though aware that his tongue was running away with him. The burning light died out of his eyes, and he laughed shortly. "And back in England they think what a nice, pleasant young man—and smile kindly on me!"

Armand flushed. They were almost the identical words his aunt had used. "Does . . . does Vyv know . . . of all this?"

"Good God, no!" Dan stared. "He hasn't the brains to see aught but what is under his nose. He sees it all as great sport, to be kept secret at all costs. No, Vyv is the best cover I could have, for who would ever suspect him—or his dearest friend—of intrigue! And *you* will not disabuse him, boy."

He jabbed the air with a menacing finger. "In fact, Armand de Brussec, I am going to spell it out for you so that there may be no misunderstandings: from this moment you will breathe no word of what you have seen or heard these past days."

"Mon Dieu! Is it likely that I would boast?" Armand's voice shook with scorn. "I am not so proud of myself!"

"Nonetheless, I repeat, you will speak to no one—least of all your sister. I'll not have my pitch queered there too."

Armand sat up abruptly—and winced. "You will please to leave Madalena alone. . . ."

"But I do not please, my dear boy. I have every intention of pursuing my interest with your sister; why else do you suppose I have been at such pains to cultivate your friendship? For the sake of your *beaux yeux?*" The young boy flushed and turned pale. "I admit I was a damn fool to involve you in this venture, but I had no idea you were so riddled with scruples, and it's no use repining.

"But I do urge you to consider most carefully, for I make you a promise that if the least suspicion attaches itself to me, it will likewise attach to you. Not only would the ensuing scandal devolve ruinously upon your uncle and aunt, who have been so good to you—it would almost certainly result in immediate expulsion from England for both you and your sister!"

Chapter 9

MADALENA WAS SURPRISED to hear a sound from within her brother's room. After a moment's hesitation she tapped lightly on the door and went in.

Armand was sitting on the edge of the bed, facing the window. Apart from a single nervous jerk of the head as she entered, he made no attempt to greet her.

"Armand, *mon cher!* No one said that you were returned!"

Undeterred by his silence, Madalena bounced onto the bed beside him, not noticing how he flinched with the sudden movement.

"We have only just arrived ourselves, you know," she chattered on, "and oh, how it makes one stiff to be sitting in a chaise for so long. Our poor aunt—she is quite prostrate and is gone to lie down . . . and Phoebe must be pining for her John, for she has spoken hardly a word on the way home. I must tell you, we had the most dreadful quarrel, and for days I was not popular, but all is now well."

She sprang suddenly to her feet. "Oh, but the time we have had! It will take me an age to tell it all to you, for you will never guess whom we met."

In her excitement, she put out a hand to grasp her brother, and was totally unprepared for the violence of his reaction.

"Non! Ne me touche pas!"

"Armand! What is wrong? Are you ill?" Madalena looked more closely and noticed for the first time his extreme pallor, the tight-drawn line of his mouth. *"Ah, mon pauvre!* You *are* ill!"

"I am all right," he muttered through shut teeth. "Just go and leave me alone."

"Indeed I will not! A fine sister that would make of me!"

His eyes closed in a kind of weary despair, and she sank at once to her knees beside him, her own stiffness forgotten. "Oh, come, now!" she coaxed him. "It is only your own Maddie. Tell me, I implore you. You know how stubborn I can be. . . . I do not mean to leave until I know what it is that troubles you so."

Armand made a curious choking sound, halfway between a laugh and a groan. *"Dieu*—why do I bother!" He turned a little, so that his right side became visible to her, exposing the torn sleeve and the makeshift bandage.

Madalena exclaimed in horror and demanded to know how he had come by such an injury.

"No fuss, Maddie—I beg you! It is a scratch only."

"As to that, we must without a doubt remove your coat at once so that I may see this scratch." Alternately coaxing and bullying, she eased him out of the coat, her eyes flying constantly to his face lest she should be hurting him.

Her fingers struggled with the complex knot Sir Vyvian had wrought, while her tongue scolded. "I said, did I not, how all this gallivanting with Daniel would come to no good. Oh, I shall have much to say to him when next I see him . . . to let you travel in such a state!"

The handkerchief came away at last. She drew a sharp breath.

"*Dieu me sauve!* We must take this arm at once to Dr. Laidlaw!"

A sudden bout of coughing seized Armand, culminating in a groan.

"No!" His voice was faint, and Madalena saw that he was now very white about the mouth. She hurriedly piled the pillows into a heap and made him lie back. She slipped from the room and returned almost at once with a generous measure of the brigadier's finest brandy.

He gulped it down, and Madalena watched anxiously until a little color came back into his face.

She sighed. "That is better. Now, my brother, do you feel able to make the effort, or shall I send for Dr. Laidlaw to come to you here, for one way or another I am determined that you shall see him. It needs only a chill to descend on your lungs—"

"*Stupide!* I'll not have Tante Esmé or anyone else asking awkward questions."

She stared back mulishly.

"Oh, very well, if I must, then I will go to Laidlaw—but I do not see the necessity. It needs only a fresh bandage."

Armand's manner remained petulant, but he allowed his sister to tie a clean handkerchief around the wound and help him into a loose-fitting coat.

She smuggled him down the stairs and out to the stables without incident. There she instructed a broadly grinning, blatantly curious Jamie to harness Betsy to the gig.

Armand said little as they set off at a somewhat erratic trot. To own the truth, he was bone-weary and his arm throbbed abominably with every jolt of the wheels in the ruts of the driveway.

It had been an exhausting ride home. He doubted he

would have accomplished it at all had not Vyv insisted on accompanying him for the greater part of the way. Vyv had been uncharacteristically quiet, and Armand wondered how much he had been shaken by Daniel's behavior. He was not of great intelligence, but neither was he stupid.

The unexpectedness of Dan's treachery, his utter callousness, still haunted him, nagging as the pain in his arm nagged.

"Madalena?"

Something in his voice made her look at him.

"How do you feel about Daniel? Truthfully?"

Her eyes sparked. "At this moment, I think it is very well that he is not here!"

"But leaving this moment aside?"

Madalena considered. "He is very amusing, I think, and he has great charm." She grinned suddenly. "I believe he is a little in love with me."

She didn't notice her brother's sudden tenseness.

"And you, Maddie? How do you feel? It is important."

Her laugh rang out. "Me? In love with Daniel? Is that what you think?"

When Armand didn't answer, she glanced at his pensive face and exlaimed, "You have quarreled! There has been a fight! But of course! That is why you were so . . . *bouleversé*—you did not wish me to know! Now I can see it all. It is Daniel who is responsible for your injury!"

In her excitement, Madalena jerked on the rein, and the gig swerved sharply to the side of the road.

"Maddie! For pity's sake! You will land us in the ditch. Give me the reins."

"Certainly not!" she retorted, quickly reestablishing control of Betsy. "I am very well able to manage, as you can see. And I am right, am I not?"

Armand shifted uncomfortably. "I . . . there was some trouble . . . a slight accident, that is all. I cannot explain."

"Oh, *parbleu!* Always it is the same with you men! Al-

ways the great mystery—the secret you cannot divulge.
Well, I can tell you that I find you all stupid and quite
boring!"

She drove on in mutinous silence. It was true. These
men were nothing but a trouble to her! It was not enough
that Papa, with all his great wisdom, was so quixotic as to
imagine that he could castigate the emperor and not suffer
for it. Now, here was Armand playing at goodness knows
what folly! And as for Devereux—only the *bon Dieu* knew
how deep in intrigue he was! Her heart lurched, and she
was immediately angry—what Devereux did was of no
interest to her. He would please himself! The doctor's
house loomed up through her tears, and she brought the
gig to an unnecessarily abrupt halt.

Dr. Laidlaw subjected them both to a few searching
looks as he tutted over the injury, but since neither seemed
disposed to enlighten him, he held his peace. When
Armand again began to cough, however, he was quite
adamant that the boy must take a few days in bed. Madalena expected him to demur, but the quiet sympathy of Dr.
Laidlaw's daughter, Sally, who had been assisting her
father, had acted like a balm upon Armand's bruised
spirits, and he gave in, insisting only that his aunt should
know nothing of his injured arm.

When the time passed and there was no word from
Daniel, Madalena supposed that they had indeed quarreled. It seemed a pity, but no amount of probing would
induce Armand to speak of it, and then the mystery was
driven from her mind.

The duchess was failing. Madalena could not fool herself. This time, unless there was some miracle wrought,
her dear friend could not possibly rally.

Throughout the long summer days Madalena spent
every available moment at her side, always ready with a
smile and a softly spoken word when the duchess roused
from a heavily drugged sleep; for the rest, she sat quietly

stitching or just staring before her with folded hands, while her heart grew every day more like a stone in her breast.

Sometimes Dev would be there to bully her into taking fresh air and exercise. It was enough, he had insisted with considerable dryness, that her aunt should be on his back already for permitting her to assume duties that were arduous and quite unsuited to a sensitive young girl. He did not add that Mrs. Vernon had most forcibly, and with none of her customary vagueness, expressed it as her opinion that Madalena had already endured more than could be thought tolerable in the early loss of her mama—not to mention being separated from the father she so adored—without being subjected to further distress.

The duke wholeheartedly agreed with her, but wondered how one prevented Madalena from doing anything upon which she had set her heart.

As if to confirm this, Madalena now sighed. "Poor Tante—she cannot see that it is what I wish. True love and friendship do not permit one to take only the happiness."

She spread her hands expressively. "How am I expected to think only of Phoebe's bridal clothes at such a time? And what of poor Miss Payne—am I to abandon her?"

That faithful and devoted lady, who had nursed her dear charge for so long, and with such constancy, had come more and more to depend upon Madalena's youth and resilience of character in these last troubled days, and Madalena's comings and goings were by now so accepted by the entire household that she had taken to entering the house most mornings through the open windows of the library, without troubling anyone to answer the door.

On a morning that was already hot and promised to be hotter, she heard sounds of movement from the small room adjoining the library, a room she had once laughingly dubbed Dev's *cabinet de travail*.

Thinking him to be there, she stepped across to bid him good morning.

She knocked, pushed the door wider, and was puzzled to find the room apparently empty. She turned to leave, and was instantly aware of a stealthy movement behind the door. Sensing an intruder, Madalena opened her mouth to summon help, but before she could utter a sound, a hand was clamped tight across her mouth. She struggled vainly against an arm locked about her body like a vice, and then suddenly she was quite still, her eye riveted upon that arm, for—merciful heaven!—it was wearing a familiar blue uniform sleeve.

She made frantic squeaking noises, twisting her head until a voice she knew breathed furiously in her ear.

"Silence, little termagant! I am going to release you now, but make me a scene, and be sure I will snap that pretty neck!"

The hands slackened. Madalena shrugged herself free and spun around, bristling with indignation, to confront Gaston Marceau.

"*Sacre mille diables!* Madalena de Brussec!"

"*Oui, mon brave capitaine!*" she panted scathingly. "It is indeed me . . . and I should be very much interested to know how you come to be in this house, where you do not at all belong." She clapped a hand to her mouth. "*Tiens!* You are broke-parole . . . oh no!" She peered around. "Paul is not . . . ?"

"No." Captain Marceau had recovered swiftly from his initial dismay on seeing Madalena. He whispered now with a hint of exaggerated irony, "Be easy. I am quite alone! So . . . what would you? Am I to be surrendered to the law? Can you do that to a fellow countryman?"

"*Sot!* Be quiet and I will think!"

Madalena's mind was racing over possibilities. Of course he must not be caught . . . somehow she must get him away. But how? *Voyons*—there was Dev's boat, the *Seamew*. If Gaston could only sail her. . . . Dev would be very angry, of course, if he ever found out, but if it were just to vanish . . .

Gaston Marceau watched the so-revealing face before him, delighting again in its myriad changing expressions, remembering how that overgenerous mouth, now pursed in fierce concentration, could curve into instant laughter, setting the eyes brimming with golden light. Were it not for this accursed war, he might have enjoyed pursuing their relationship to a more intimate conclusion. As things were . . .

"You appear to be familiar with your surroundings," he said abruptly. "Are you, then, related to Lytten?"

"No," she replied absently. "I come each day to visit his . . ." Her voice trailed away as the full implication of his words hit her. "What did you say?"

He did not answer at once, and she grasped urgently at his sleeve. "Captain Marceau, I insist that you tell me! Are you an intruder in this house—or is it that you are here . . . by arrangement?" Even as she uttered the words, she knew, and the blood drained from her face. Dev running an escape route for prisoners of war! She knew that such organizations existed, but Dev! Oh, it was madness, for if he were discovered . . . How was treason—her mind shrank from the terrible word—punishable here in England? In France there was Madame Guillotine. . . .

"Are you unwell, mademoiselle?"

Captain Marceau's voice came to her from a great distance. Madalena strove to still her wild imaginings. "It is nothing," she said.

"I was about to ask if you could contrive to forget this meeting." His eyebrow quirked almost sheepishly. "The fact is, Mademoiselle Madalena, I should not have shown myself."

Unaware that each word brought fresh torture to Madalena, he walked swiftly across to the paneling and turned a candle bracket. There was a soft whirring, and one of the panels slid back.

"I am supposed to lie concealed here," he confessed ruefully. "Ingenious, is it not? But, *parbleu,* so stuffy! One must breathe, after all. I fear, however, that Monsieur le duc would not appreciate my necessity."

Madalena swallowed to relieve the curious constriction in her throat. "I shall say nothing. But I advise that you return to your hiding place with all speed, monsieur, and resign yourself to its discomforts. You may be less fortunate if you are discovered a second time."

Gaston took one of her hands, and found it cold in spite of the warm day. He raised it to his lips, his restless eyes never once leaving her face. "A thousand pardons, mademoiselle, that I used you so ill. Perchance, if I am spared, I may one day be permitted to make amends."

Without warning, he bent suddenly and just touched his lips to hers—and then he was gone and the panel was sliding into place.

Madalena turned as in a dream and walked with lagging steps back through the library and up the staircase. She was very quiet for the remainder of the day, and when, toward evening, the invalid's blurred eyes fluttered open, they were able to discern the rigidity of the slight figure at her side—head bent and hands clasped convulsively upon the coverlet. Her own hand groped feebly to cover those clasped ones.

Madalena was instantly concerned. *"Chérie*—there is something you want?"

The head moved feebly on the pillows; Madalena had to bend close to catch the words. "Do not grieve, child . . . if it is the will of the *bon Dieu,* I am well content." There was a long-drawn sigh. "It has been so . . . long."

Madalena choked back her tears. "Oh, but you must not leave me . . . not now. . . . I need you . . . I don't know how I shall go on without you!"

A vague look of distress flared for a brief moment in the weary eyes, and then they quietly closed.

Madalena knew a moment of sheer terror; she pulled on the bell rope until Miss Payne came running, and from then onward there was much subdued coming and going. Dr. Laidlaw arrived, and after examining the duchess, spoke to Lytten in hushed tones, his manner grave.

Devereux came to Madalena's side and took her arm gently but firmly. "Come, I am taking you home."

She stiffened, staring in a panic from him to the still figure so tiny beneath the pink silk counterpane.

"No! I must stay. I . . . she might need me!"

"She is not conscious, my dear, and Dr. Laidlaw assures me she will remain that way for some hours."

Her mouth trembled mutinously, and his voice took on a sterner note. "I am quite determined, Maddie. You have been here all day—you are worn out!"

The doctor joined them. "His grace speaks the truth, mademoiselle. I promise you, there is no more you can do for the moment, and we cannot have you ill upon our hands also." He smiled down at her in his gently quizzical fashion. "I should not be able to face your good aunt."

With a last, lingering glance for her dear friend, Madalena allowed herself to be led unresisting from the room and down the staircase. Castor and Pollux rose from their places before the great fireplace and ambled across the hall, but they, too, seemed subdued, and contented themselves with nuzzling her hand.

She spoke no word for the whole of the journey. Devereux finally reined in the horses.

"Madalena . . ."

"She is going to die, isn't she?"

He looked at her white, shuttered face and knew there was little he could say for comfort. He took her hand, and it lay passive in his own. "Yes," he said quietly. "I'm afraid she is."

"I should have been permitted to stay."

"No, Madalena. It could be many hours." Deliberately he kept his voice even. "It is impossible to tell . . . how long."

"I begin to think that you do not care," Madalena said in flat, precise tones.

Devereux's hand tightened on hers, until she cried out with the pain. Slowly, great shuddering sobs welled up and tore at her throat, until they engulfed her. Devereux caught her close, pressing her head tight against his shoulder, his fingers moving in the red-gold curls while tears soaked into his coat.

In her distress and confusion, the imminent death of his mama had somehow become inextricably linked with his own dangerous folly, and she wept for them both. "Ah . . . ah . . . forgive me. I did not mean . . ."

"It's all right, *petite*," he soothed, unaware of the conflict raging inside her. "Hush, now . . . you must let her go, you know."

"I know it." Madalena gasped between sobs. "Oh, I am selfish!"

Presently she sat back. Apart from an occasional convulsive shudder, her grief was spent. Like a child, she allowed Dev to mop up her tears, and finally gave a prosaic little sniff.

"*Ah, mon Dieu*—what an exhibition I make of myself!" She put out a shaky hand. "And your poor coat—it is quite ruined!" Without looking up, she added haltingly, "Dev . . . I am so ashamed . . . to have spoken as I did."

"Good God! Do you think I care anything about that!" He bit off the words and continued more gently, almost to himself. "I have lived with it for so long now, watched her go from a beautiful, vital woman to a shell. There is a kind of relief in knowing it is almost at an end. Can you understand that?"

"Oh, yes!" She longed to comfort him, but sensed that

he would hate it, so she said simply, "You will let me know? I promise I shall not make you another scene."

The ladies were still at breakfast on the following morning when the crunch of wheels was heard on the driveway. Madalena pushed her plate away with a nervous gesture, the bread upon it already mangled beyond recognition.

When Devereux was admitted, she was standing, pale but fully composed. Only the whiteness of her knuckles gripping the back of the chair betrayed her distress.

He halted upon the threshold and apologized for intruding upon their meal, but Mrs. Vernon, guessing from one look at his face what must be the purpose of so early a call, assured him with gentle concern that he must not be thinking any such thing.

"Your dear mama?" She hesitantly voiced the question that Madalena could not ask.

"This morning, ma'am, very peacefully—at about five o'clock."

The duke's words, conventionally phrased, were addressed to Mrs. Vernon, but all his attention was concentrated upon her niece. Dear God—how still she was! Her plain-ugly little face was heavy-eyed with lack of sleep. Feeling an overwhelming urge to ease her hurt, he found himself saying abruptly, "Madalena, will you come back with me now?"

Mrs. Vernon's halting but very genuine commiserations were stemmed in mid-flow; her mouth dropped open, and both she and Phoebe exclaimed aloud at the seeming insensitivity of such a suggestion.

Their words fell on the empty air.

Devereux held out a hand, and with only a moment's hesitation Madalena placed her own trembling one into its comforting clasp. He returned her uncertain gaze with a quiet, confident nod.

When, however, she stood before the door of the duchess's room, she turned to him in sudden panic.

"I can't go in!"

"Yes you can. Come." He held the door wide and gently propelled her forward.

She had no idea what she had expected or dreaded. Here there was only the soft light from the branched candles at the head of the bed, and banks of white flowers that filled the air with an incredible sweetness.

Madalena found herself drawn irresistibly toward the bed, and scarcely heard Dev murmur that he would wait below.

The duchess lay in a simple white gown beneath the silken coverlet. Her hair had been brushed loose and bound into braids with white ribbons; it framed a face so serene that Madalena drew closer to gaze in awe. The lines of suffering had gone, and she looked as she must have looked in the days before ill health overtook her. It was an unbelievable transformation. Madalena lost all sense of time; she sat beside the bed as she had so often done, and it was as though her dear friend was with her still, giving her strength and a great feeling of peace, almost of happiness. It was only with reluctance that she finally crept from the room and made her way downstairs.

The library door was ajar. She walked in—and stopped, her heart turning over.

Dev was leaning against the mantelshelf, his head bowed in so obvious an abandonment to grief that Madalena experienced a fierce, almost maternal longing to gather him into the comfort of her arms. But such grief for a man is a private thing, as she well knew, and so she silently stepped back into the hall, where she made a point of speaking quite loudly and at some length to the dogs before she again approached the library and tapped lightly on the door.

Dev had moved to the window, and turned as she came

in. An anxious look reassured her that he had recovered himself.

"Thank you for bringing me," she said simply. "It is, of all things, a memory that I shall treasure."

"I am glad." The strain in his voice hurt her.

"How did you know that it was just the right thing for me?"

He put a hand beneath her chin and turned her grave, funny little face up to him. "I am beginning to realize that I know you as I know myself."

She stood quiescent under his brooding, intense scrutiny, her widening eyes returning just the hint of a query. He shook his head at last and said on a sigh, "Come, I will take you home."

It was a simple funeral, and when it was over, Devereux came briefly to the house. He would be going away for a while, he said. Miss Payne had gone into Devonshire almost at once, to a married sister. She had been offered a home at Lytten Manor for as long as she wished, but Miss Payne had always been somewhat in awe of her austere cousin, and without her dear Dominique the house held too many memories. She had been quite overwhelmed to discover that the duchess had left her an annuity sufficient to make her independent, and so she had stammered her gratitude and departed in a flood of tears immediately after the funeral.

Devereux brought for Madalena her little statuette, and also the picture of the Madonna that had hung beside the duchess's bed, which she had so admired. With it was a note in the duchess's hand.

When Devereux had gone, she took them up to the privacy of her own room, where she opened the letter.

It was brief—no more than a few lines in a shaky, yet elegant hand; Madalena fancied she could hear the gentle voice framing the words. *"Ma chère,"* it ran, "I am leaving to you my picture, which you so admired, as a remembrance. It is impossible for me to write what you have brought to my life these last months. Such deep and abiding joy cannot be measured. Do not grieve for me, for be assured that I shall always be near to you. . . ."

There was more—something about Devereux—but Madalena's eyes had blurred, and she could not read it.

She folded the letter and laid it neatly away with the statuette in a drawer beneath a pile of clothes. Then she closed the drawer with a dreadful feeling of finality, leaving only the picture to be hung above her bed.

Chapter 10

PHOEBE WAS MARRIED in late October and was soon blissfully installed in a little house not far from John's parents. Madalena had not expected to miss Phoebe so much, but though Armand rode with her most mornings, he had become very much taken with the idea of becoming a doctor and spent most of his days at the Laidlaws, so that she was thrown very much back on her own resources. She too was always welcome at the Laidlaws, but much as she liked Sally, her undiluted company was a trial.

The fact was, Madalena was missing the duchess keenly—and not only the duchess. She had seen Dev only once—and that briefly—since the day of the funeral, and her heart ached for a sight of him.

Daniel, they had seen only once also. He had put in a brief appearance during the late summer. It was a visit charged with an uncomfortable atmosphere and ending in disaster.

Mrs. Vernon, showing a distinct lack of perception, had insisted upon his staying for a night or two, convinced that not only must Armand be pleased to see his friend, but that his visit was just what was needed to lift Madalena out of the lowness of spirits occasioned by the duchess's death.

Since the conquest of Madalena was the sole object of his visit, Daniel Merchent had ignored Armand's hostility and had set himself, with practiced ease, to the task of making himself agreeable to her.

Mrs. Vernon, her mind already full of bridals, began to cherish notions that this nice young man was becoming serious in his attachment to her niece. Of course, it would be necessary to obtain Etienne's consent, but even Hortense had had no fault to find with either Mr. Merchent's connections or his prospects; she was persuaded that it was a match Madalena's father could not but approve.

And so, basking in the warmth of Mrs. Vernon's approbation, and further encouraged by Madalena, who overcompensated for Armand's fit of the sullens by being spontaneously generous in her attention to him, Daniel suddenly threw discretion aside and declared his passion —begged her to marry him.

Madalena was stunned! She stammered a blank refusal and watched the color flood the fair, intense face as disbelief turned slowly to mortification and then to anger. *Peste!* If she had not been so preoccupied, she must have seen the signs, and could then have steered him away from so precipitate a proposal!

As things were, he took it hard. He left almost at once, leaving Madalena distressed, Armand vastly relieved, and Mrs. Vernon tearful. Fortunately, however, Phoebe's wedding was soon upon them, and there was little time for morbid reflection.

Kit came home when the preparations were at their height, and stayed several weeks, providing Madalena with just the required anodyne—a protective, unquestioning affection that demanded no more of her than that she should be herself.

Had she but known it, Kit was more than ready to lay his heart—his very life, if need be—at her feet, but he knew that, for her, only one man existed; he was content to remain her devoted cousin, friend, and when necessary, confidant.

He took his mother quietly to task over the business of Daniel Merchent, pointing out the futility of such scheming, an accusation that caused his mama's breast to swell with indignation. It was an extraordinary thing, she had bridled, that her son, who spent most of his time in London, should feel himself better qualified to gauge his cousin's innermost feelings than she, who saw Madalena every day!

"For it may surprise you to know, Kit, that the child has not so much as mentioned Lytten since his mama passed away. I am persuaded that she has put him quite out of her mind!"

Kit gave up. Useless to attempt to convince her that Madalena's reticence was a matter for disquiet.

But now Kit had returned to London, and when Madalena was not with Armand or Sally, she would take long solitary walks, assuring her aunt that trudging through sodden leaves was of all things what she enjoyed doing. More often than not her steps took her in the direction they had so often taken in the past.

So it was that, on a bleak November day, she stepped out onto the carriageway near Lytten Manor, to be joyously greeted by Castor and Pollux. Heedless of the damp ground, she knelt to hug them; rough, eager tongues licked at her face, heavy tails thumping back and forth.

The horses were almost upon her before she saw them. Devereux, leaner and more saturnine than she had remembered, sat astride Thunderer, and at his side, coolly elegant in a flowing habit of rich crimson, a dashing hat perched at a becoming angle on glistening dark curls, was Lady Serena Fairfax. The amused smile kindling her worldly wise eyes was reflected in her low, musical voice.

"Why, it is our little *émigrée!* How delightful to see you, my dear, and how . . . unexpected!"

Madalena struggled to stand erect, but the dogs impeded her. Devereux dismounted and called them to heel. They backed off with reluctance and sat, their tails still thumping the ground.

Devereux lifted Madalena up and brushed the damp leaves and twigs from her soft brown pelisse. Her bonnet had slipped a little to one side; without speaking, he straightened it, and tucking away a stray red-gold curl, secured the ribbons, subjecting her as he did so to a minute examination.

Disconcerted by the presence of Lady Serena, Madalena stammered incoherently, *"Pardon* . . . I did not know . . . sometimes I walk here . . . but I would not intrude . . ."

Devereux silenced her, holding her when she would have turned away. "Foolish one! You must know you are free to go wherever you choose."

Her eyes were intent upon him, as though she would treasure up every feature and store it away.

At last she withdrew from his clasp. He caught at her hand and said with low urgency, "You are . . . all right?"

She nodded. Their eyes held for a moment longer, and then he let her go. The murmur of voices floated back to her as she stumbled along the path—voices, and the sound of a husky, very feminine laugh. . . .

It was as Christmas approached that Madalena felt the absence of her father most keenly, but Kit came home again, and Phoebe and John braved the inclement weather to join the family gathering, so that it became impossible for her not to enjoy the festivities.

When Phoebe arrived, the two girls exchanged a rapturous embrace, and soon Madalena was carrying Phoebe off to her room, where Phoebe's newfound dignity soon deserted her and they fell to chattering like a couple of magpies.

"You are happy with your John, my Phoebe? Ah, yes, I can see it—there is a glow about you!"

"Oh, indeed, it is prodigious fine to be a married lady!" exclaimed Phoebe. She jumped up and went to the window, and then turned, her cheeks rather pink. "Maddie? Can you keep a secret?"

Madalena looked at her and clapped her hands. *"Voyons!* I have guessed it! You are *enceinte, n'est-ce pas?"*

She rushed across to envelop her cousin in an enthusiastic hug. "You—to be a mother! It does not seem possible!"

"Maddie, do hush! I have not yet told Mama. You mustn't breathe a word until I have done so."

The news, when told, was celebrated in fine style, and the time flew past.

It was on a bitter morning at the end of December that Daniel Merchent appeared again. The family had driven out en masse to return Christmas calls—all but Madalena, who had kept to her room with a slight cold.

It was there that Armand sought her out. His face was ashen, and she pulled him quickly inside and shut the door. "Armand, are you ill? Why do you look like this?"

"Dan Merchent is here. I met him as I was riding back from the Laidlaws'. He is downstairs waiting to see you."

"Peste—I do not wish to see him. You can say that I am very ill."

"Maddie, you must see him!" Armand stood tense, his

back against the door, and something in his voice sent a small shiver of apprehension through her.

"Something is badly wrong. You will please to tell me."

Armand was silent for so long that she almost screamed. And then, in an unsteady voice, he began. "Dan has news . . . out of France. I . . . . he says Papa has been arrested."

"Dieu!" The room swayed, and Madalena sat down abruptly on the bed. "So, it has come at last."

Armand slumped beside her; without speaking, like children seeking comfort, they clasped hands.

"Did he . . . say what happened?" Madalena asked at last.

"No—I did not ask. He was most insistent that he should see you."

"Then he shall see me."

In the little morning room, Daniel Merchent turned from the window.

Madalena launched at once into speech. "Is it true —what you have said? For it seems to me very strange that you should know such a thing!"

"There is no mistake, I promise you." Daniel's voice was harsh, uncompromising. "Your father is in La Force —after a highly inflammatory speech condemning his emperor and the entire disastrous Russian campaign."

Madalena shut her eyes. *It would be true. Oh, without a doubt, it would be true!*

Daniel Merchent observed her reactions closely and seemed strangely pleased with what he saw.

"Your father means a lot to you?"

"I would die for him gladly!" Madalena declared passionately.

"I hardly think that such a drastic sacrifice will be called for." Daniel's voice was smooth. "However, a few weeks ago I made you a proposal which you were pleased to scorn . . ."

He paused, watching her with narrowed eyes. Armand,

suddenly realizing what was to come, started forward with a cry.

"If," Daniel continued, as though Armand did not exist, "you were now prepared to reconsider your answer, I for my part would guarantee to arrange for your father's escape."

Madalena stood very still and straight. She was dimly aware of Armand beside her, urging her not to make any such bargain. In a detached way she even found time to wonder how she could ever have thought Daniel attractive. Truly, the eyes were of a hardness, the mouth cruel.

"So, monsieur, I am to sell myself to you in return for my father's freedom. This is what you are suggesting?"

Daniel Merchent's mouth tightened into a thin line. "I would hardly call it selling yourself, mademoiselle; I am still prepared to offer you marriage—a generous offer in the circumstances. I am sure you will appreciate that I might well demand less . . . happy terms?"

Her look scorned him. "I make you my thanks! But since I do not in the least wish to marry you, your terms are of little interest to me."

He flushed. "A brave show of insolence, my dear, but you would do well to weigh your words with more care. How will they sound, think you, when your father's head rolls in a basket?"

Madalena gasped, her lips grown curiously stiff. "The emperor would never . . ."

"Would he not! Etienne de Brussec has been a thorn in his side for long enough; he is not likely to show him much mercy now."

Armand put a swift arm around his sister as she swayed, his own face only a little less ghastly than hers.

"Leave her alone, Merchent! *Sang Dieu!* Have you no pity?"

"Pity is a useless emotion, boy—fit only for fools and weaklings." Daniel Merchent set his hat on his head and picked up his gloves. The lash of his riding whip jerked through nervous fingers. "You have until noon tomorrow. I stay overnight at the inn in the village. Perhaps, Madalena, you will be good enough to convey your answer to me there."

His hand was already on the door when Madalena's voice halted him. Her face was bloodless. Only her eyes blazed with the unbearable agony of her decision.

"I will not trouble you to wait for your answer, Daniel. It is no!" She forced the word out, and her voice steadied. "I do not ask how you came by your information, for it seems to me that such knowledge could well come from dishonorable sources."

She thought of Dev, and for a moment she almost wavered. "You do not, I think, know my father, but I will tell you now that, of a certainty, he would never accept his freedom on such terms as you have laid down."

Armand's sharply drawn breath was almost a sob.

Daniel Merchent shot her a venomous look; the whip jerked once more through his hand. "Then God help him!" he flung at her, and strode from the room. A moment later the hall door slammed, reverberating through the house.

"Amen!" whispered Madalena piteously. She began to shake, so that Armand had to hold her tight.

"Stop it, Maddie! *Ah, ma pauvre,* I beseech you to calm yourself, or you will be ill. We shall think of something."

"Say you do not blame me, that I did not agree—"

"Agree! To such a monstrous suggestion!" Armand exploded with feeling. "I tell you, you do not know that man as I do; someday I will tell you! We do not even know that he speaks the truth."

"No—it is true." Madalena sighed and touched her breast. "I feel it here."

"*Voyons*—then I will go myself to France. There are still many people who love Papa enough to help us."

Madalena sprang up, suddenly resolute. "That is madness! No, no, it is clear that I must see Devereux without delay."

"Lytten?" Armand stared. "Why Lytten? How can he do anything?"

Like a whirlwind, Madalena was almost through the door. "I cannot explain, but he will help, I know he will! Promise me that you will do nothing foolish, my Armand . . . and say nothing to the family, I beg you!"

Within a very short space of time Madalena had dragged on her riding habit and was riding furiously toward Lytten Manor.

Tom, the young footman, was delighted to see the little mam'selle again. The stooping figure of Gaston appeared, and in answer to her urgent query he was obliged to inform her that his grace was from home.

Tom could not help noticing how the brightness dimmed in the girl's face—and wondered at it. There had been much speculation below stairs; the house had been an empty place since their dear duchess's death had deprived them of the little missy's visits, and the hope that the duke would take her to wife seemed, by now, doomed to disappointment. Still, p'raps there was hope after all. . . .

Gaston was saying kindly, "We are expecting his grace to return sometime this evening, probably late, mademoiselle. I will tell him of your visit. He will doubtless call on you."

"No . . . no!" She saw their surprised faces. "I will call again myself tomorrow."

When night came and all had long since retired, Madalena was still tossing. How difficult it all was. If only Armand would be patient a little longer. . . . She had tried to reassure him. She tried to compose herself, but sleep would not come. She banged her pillow crossly. *"Tiens,* it is of no use—you are like one big lump of lead!"

Throwing back the blankets, she padded across to the

window; already it was thickly crusted with frost. She rubbed vigorously at the pane, her face pressed to the icy surface, her eyes straining in the direction of Lytten Manor. . . .

It was well past midnight when Devereux let himself quietly into the house. A dozing footman sprang to attention and relieved his grace of hat, gloves, whip, and finally the all-enveloping greatcoat. He wondered whether his grace would be requiring refreshment, it being a rare frosty night to have been on the road. Devereux moved to the staircase. "I require only one thing—and that is my bed." He turned. "But you may remove my boots, if you would make yourself useful. I doubt I can raise the energy."

The household, being well used to his odd comings and goings, had been well trained. Even his valet was not permitted to wait up for him.

In his room a welcome fire blazed in the grate, and brandy decanter and glass were set in readiness upon a small side table.

Devereux poured a generous measure and stretched out on the bed with a thankful sigh. The last few days had been more than usually trying; there was little joy in crossing the channel at this time of year. But it would have to be attempted at least one more time.

He drew a letter from his pocket and weighed it thoughtfully in his hand—a letter he had carried from Hartwell, where the exiled court of Louis XVIII was established. He would give much to know what the old Archbishop of Rheims, Louis's chief chaplain, had written in reply to the letter brought by Devereux from Prince Talleyrand. He had certainly been overjoyed to receive word from his illustrious nephew, and seemed to see in it a sign that the prodigal was at last acknowledging the error of his ways.

Devereux's lips twitched, remembering how different

had been corpulent Louis's reaction to Prince Talleyrand's apparent change of heart. He had remarked with
some malice that Bonaparte must be nearing his end, for
when the Directory had been in similar straits, the then
Monsieur Talleyrand had written in like manner to the
"little corporal." The king had then bent an acid smile
upon the old prelate and concluded, "If you are replying
to the letter, my dear archbishop, pray tell the prince
that I accept the auger of his good memory!"

Well, here was the reply; Devereux opened a small
drawer beside the bed, tossed the letter inside, and
locked it again. He sighed and stood up, wondering what
the devil he was to tell Madalena of the other matter that
filled his thoughts.

A sound—a kind of creaking—froze him in the act
of removing his coat. It came from somewhere near the
fireplace. With infinite care he slid a pistol from his
pocket, cocked it, and said in a clear, hard voice, "Come
out, if you please—and without any tricks, or you are
dead."

There was a moment of silence, and then a smothered
Gallic curse from the depths of the leather armchair was
followed by a familiar aggrieved muttering. "I would be
very glad to come out, I promise you, but you have been
so long in coming that I have gone to sleep with the fire—
and now I have a crick in the neck, and besides, I am
entirely stiff!"

Devereux laid down the pistol and strode across the
room. He seized the chair and swung it around. Amber
eyes, heavy with sleep, blinked up at him from the folds
of a deep blue cloak. As Madalena struggled to extricate
herself, he seemed to swoop down on her, freeing her and
bringing her, in one movement, to her feet. She grimaced
and tried a few hobbling steps, coming back at last to
where he stood—a rather grim figure with folded arms.

"Well, Madalena. I am awaiting your explanation."

"You are angry?"

"Yes, I rather think I am."

She wrinkled her nose at him. "It is because you think it not *convenable* for me to be here. But I used the library window, and nobody has seen me. I meant to come to you in the morning, but then I could not wait!"

A note of urgency, almost of despair, had crept into her voice, so that he put a hand beneath her chin to turn her face to the light. "Something is wrong, little one?"

The words trembled very slightly. "It is Papa—he is in prison."

Devereux gave her an odd look, but she was too distraught to notice. "How do you know this?"

It all came out then, the words tumbling over themselves as she lapsed from time to time into her mother tongue—Armand's involvement with the smuggling, which he had finally confessed, Daniel's ultimatum. . . .

Devereux listened, and with each moment his suspicions about Daniel Merchent hardened into certainty. All the investigations he had set in motion with regard to the smuggling had seemed to lead back to Merchent, but he had so far failed to uncover the size and scope of the operation. To have known so quickly of De Brussec's arrest, to be in a position to secure his release, if indeed he could so do, indicated a connection with some powerful organization inside France—the secret police, perhaps —for whom Monsieur de Brussec's imprisonment could be more of a headache than anything else.

It would certainly seem so, if the information Devereux had had from Madame Bertha was to be believed. She had been agog with news when he had visited the *patisserie* on Christmas Eve. The streets of Paris were already seething with rumors of an uprising, she had assured him passionately. La Force should not long hold that good, kindly man—the Rue Roi de Sicile would run with blood. There was much more in similar vein, but nothing of any coherence.

It had been left to Prince Talleyrand to provide a more succinct account of events.

". . . It was inevitable, my friend. Word had it that De Brussec was already incensed by the army's appalling losses revealed in Bulletin 29. It needed only the emperor's precipitate return to Paris on the following day, with the accompanying rumors that he was bent on raising yet another army, and the fuse was lit!

"He chose his platform well—a Christmas banquet attended by everyone of importance in Paris—to deliver as scathing, as demolishing an indictment of Napoleon Bonaparte as one could wish to hear. It was masterly!"

For a moment the cold, fishlike eyes in the pallid face almost smiled, and then the prince shrugged.

"The outcome was never in doubt; our 'little man' was apoplectic with rage; the guard arrested Monsieur de Brussec within hours, and he was thrown into La Force."

Devereux had wondered what would happen.

Again the elegant shrug. "Who can tell, duke? In his right mind, the emperor would not dare to execute so popular a man of the people, but in his present mood . . ."

The words were left hanging in the air, until Devereux, feeling a sudden chill, had urged, "Could you not use your influence, your Highness?"

The prince had stared back at him in silent hauteur, his white, bejeweled hand tightening on the malacca cane.

Devereux had pressed home his point with gentle insistence. "You will allow that I have done you a not inconsiderable number of favors in these past months —worthy, perhaps, of some small return? Monsieur de Brussec's disappearance, for instance?"

The malacca cane beat an irritable tattoo upon the floor; Talleyrand's voice was frigid. "Perhaps you also have some suggestions as to how I might accomplish this miracle without incurring the emperor's wrath?"

Devereux's mouth had twitched, but he had replied gravely, "I would not presume so far, your Highness. However, Savary, your minister of police, and the prefect, Pasquier—both are counted among your friends, are they not? Neither, I think, would relish the prospect of riots, and I am assured on good authority that there would be bloody riots! They could perhaps be persuaded to suggest some solution to our dilemma?"

Madalena had by now finished her story and was watching Devereux in some anxiety. How severe was his expression! Tears threatened to choke her throat. He could not . . . he must not fail her!

"Dev?"

It was as though he had not heard her. Misinterpreting his silence, she called his name again, tugging insistently at his sleeve.

"Dev? I beseech you! If you do not help me, I do not know what I am to do! Armand talks wildly of going to France, where of a certainty he will be killed! And Papa . . ." She could not go on.

Devereux was deeply moved by her distress; indeed, he was tempted to disclose to her the plans he had made, but so much could yet go wrong, and her anguish would then be the greater.

And so he prevaricated. "What makes you think I can be of help?"

"But assuredly you can! I know that you cross the channel many times! I used to think it was just smuggling . . . and then . . ." Madalena stopped, her face flaming. Too late she realized that in her agitation she had almost betrayed her word to Gaston Marceau.

She would have turned away, but was held prisoner. When Devereux spoke, his voice had a curious inflection.

"Yes, Madalena? And then?"

Oh, Dieu! She must think quickly! Guilt made her stammer. "I . . . I found out that you h-had been in

Paris . . . when you saw Papa . . . and brought back
the little statue. . . ."

His fingers dug uncomfortably into her shoulders. "But
that is not what you were going to say, is it, child?"

She faced him squarely then, her eyes wide and luminous in the candlelight, her thick lashes spiked with un-
shed tears. *"Eh bien* . . . then I will tell you! I had not
meant that you should ever know. It is about the war
prisoners. . . ." She saw his expression and rushed on
in a blind panic. "On the day that your m-mama died, I
m-met Captain Marceau in the library. . . . He had left
your little secret room because of the heat. I already knew
him, you see, and—"

"Oh, the damned young fool!" breathed Devereux.

"Yes, but you must not blame him, for I promised that
I would say nothing . . . only me, I am not a fool." The
tears were falling now; there was a pain in her throat, but
it was not so fierce as the pain in her heart. "I have heard
of such escape routes, and suddenly it all made itself very
clear to me—your m-mysterious excursions, the way you
were able to see Papa . . ."

She could not go on. Dev's face wore the look she had
seen only twice before, and, as then, because it made
him appear a stranger, it frightened her. The skin was
drawn tight across his cheekbones, and beneath the
satyr brows, his eyes burned.

"So that is what you think of me—some kind of traitor!
Have you confided your opinions elsewhere, pray?"

"Ah no! I did not . . . I would never . . . oh, how
can you even conceive of such a thing?" Indignation
swamped her fear, and at once the tension eased.

"My apologies, infant," the duke murmured dryly. "I
should never have doubted you."

"No, you should not!" she retorted, and wondered why
his eyes glinted with sudden humor. "I do not know
what I am to think when you explain nothing. . . ."

"Not now, Madalena." He was severe again, his tone

brooking no argument. "Someday you will know all. One thing I will tell you, however, to set your mind at rest. I do not run an escape route. Gaston Marceau was . . . someone special. You must take my word on it. Now, it remains only for me to restore you to your aunt's house before you are missed."

He smoothed away the traces of tears and fastened the thick blue cloak tight against the cold. He met a glance that had grown troubled.

"Dev? You have not said . . . about Papa? Can you . . . will you help?"

His hands stilled at her throat. She felt them tighten momentarily. "I can make you no promises, Madalena —except that I will do all that is within my power. But, for God's sake, keep that brother of yours from doing anything stupid!"

Chapter 11

NEW YEAR'S EVE AT the Vernons' found a steady stream of carriages arriving to discharge a curious assortment of passengers. Mrs. Vernon had been prevailed upon by the young people to hold a masked fancy-dress ball. Her reservations as to the effect of so much excitement upon her darling Phoebe in her present delicate condition were soon set aside by Dr. Laidlaw. He thought the ball a capital idea, and announced his intention of entering fully into the spirit of the occasion.

The big room at the rear of the house was thrown open for a thorough cleaning and polishing. It was soon being festooned with streamers and paper lanterns—a noisy, often hilarious operation that seemed to involve the entire household, with the exception of the brigadier, who, coming upon them unexpectedly, viewed the upheaval with undisguised horror and came to an immediate decision that he would leave within the hour, to spend a few nights with General Fothergill at Lower Meckleton.

Madalena flung herself into the preparations with a feverish gaiety that was causing Kit a certain amount of disquiet, the more so since Armand had become morose to the point of rudeness. It was not in character for brother and sister to be so seriously at odds.

He was not to know how close the two had come to a serious clash of wills. Armand, usually so ready to let Madalena have the ordering of things, had proved uncommonly stubborn where his father's safe deliverance was concerned. An enterprise of such danger and importance, he had insisted, could be carried through only by a man, and furthermore, a man who knew France intimately. To entrust it to Lytten, who was to him an unknown quantity, seemed crazy. Madalena, unable to offer any acceptable explanation of Dev's qualifications, had stamped an angry foot and asserted that he would of a surety ruin everything if he interfered, for Dev was very much a man—and a man of great influence!

As might be supposed, Armand, already sensitive about his lack of years and experience, had deeply resented this apparent slur upon his shortcomings and had taken refuge in a fit of the sulks.

However, Madalena could never sustain a quarrel for long, and by the morning of the ball she had coaxed Armand back into a better humor, and had induced him to approach the festivities with at least some appearance of enjoyment.

"For we must not arouse suspicion, *chéri!* To tell the family would set all in a turmoil and necessitate tedious explanations about Daniel and everything. Imagine how shocked Tante would be!"

It needed a determined effort on her own part to subdue her own sick knot of apprehension whenever she considered the gravity of Papa's situation, yet Madalena would have been less than human if she had not been a little excited at the prospect of the evening ahead.

She dressed for the ball with a fine air of bravado, and stood back from the tall mirror at last, well pleased with her exertions.

"Vraiment!" she chuckled, addressing her reflection. "You are a splendid fellow, I think. Oh, but how you will shock the good Tante Esmé!"

She was wearing black velvet breeches, which, to her dismay, were beginning to grow uncommonly tight, and a fine white silk shirt purloined from Armand's wardrobe. To complete her outfit, she had raided an old trunk in one of the attics, where she had discovered a black jerkin and a floppy-brimmed hat with an extravagantly curling feather.

The jerkin was now handsomely laced up the front with crimson cord, and when Phoebe, as a sweetly charming Columbine, came softly into the room, she was scandalized to behold her graceless cousin disporting herself before the mirror, hands on hips, endeavoring to master a manly swagger.

"Maddie!" she gasped faintly. "You are never g-going downstairs like that—in breeches?"

Madalena took up her mask and struck a teasing pose. "Do you not think me a very pretty boy?"

"You are very fine, I daresay, but . . . Oh, Lordy! Mama will have a spasm! And what some of our more straitlaced guests will make of you . . ."

"Ah, bah! You exaggerate, my Phoebe—no? Then if I am not enough respectable, you will say that it is only your little French cousin who is given to eccentricity!"

However, under pressure, she agreed to raid Armand's

wardrobe yet again; he had, she knew, a short black cloak lined splendidly with crimson, which would cover the offending breeches. "Though I do not at all see the necessity," she muttered on a sigh of regret.

In Armand's room, a pirate costume lay upon the bed. Madalena felt a twinge of unease. *Stupide,* she admonished herself, he is assuredly at the Laidlaws', and will wait to accompany them. Sally Laidlaw had been helping with the preparations earlier in the day, and Armand had escorted her home. It was not unusual for him to remain with the good doctor for many hours.

When the Laidlaws arrived, however, there was no Armand. It appeared he had left them almost at once upon seeing Sally home.

Panic clawed afresh at Madalena; not caring what anyone thought, she seized Sally's arm and dragged her into the book room, where the tables were set out for cards. She stood tense, her back pressed against the door.

"Do you know where is Armand?" she implored the astonished girl. "If he has said anything at all, you must tell me!"

Sally Laidlaw was taken aback, as much by the news that Armand was missing as by the urgency of his sister's interrogation, but in her usual serene fashion she assumed that he must have some good reason.

It was monstrously uncivil of him, she agreed with mock severity—and indeed, if anyone had cause for annoyance, it was herself. She had taken a vast amount of trouble over the blue shepherdess dress, which so exactly matched her eyes—and he was not even here to admire the result. She tossed her bright gold curls and grinned. "But since he chooses to be late, I shall console myself with Kit. He makes a very fine Roman, does he not?"

Madalena managed a wan smile—and felt sick!

Sally noticed her pallor against the stark black of her extraordinary costume and rallied her gently. "Come, my dear, don't distress yourself. Young men will ever be off on some ploy; Armand will come soon!" She stopped as a thought occurred to her. "It is just possible . . ."

Madalena's head came up with pathetic eagerness.

". . . Lytten passed us on the way home this afternoon, driving those grays of his at a wicked pace. Armand did mention that he wished to see him on a matter of some urgency. Perhaps he went to the manor when he left me. Yes, you may depend upon it—they will have broached a bottle or two, and the wretch will have lost all track of time. The duke does not come to the ball, I think?"

"N-no," Madalena replied absently, sharing none of Sally's buoyant optimism. "I think he expected not to be home."

Sally tucked a friendly arm under hers. "Well, there you are, then. Your brother is almost certainly with him, and is past praying for. Let us waste no more time on him when we might be enjoying ourselves."

Madalena went through all the motions of laughing and dancing, thankful for the concealment afforded by her mask.

Why should Armand wish to see Dev, unless it were to demand to know what his plans were? Perhaps even to insist that he be included in any rescue attempt.

It needed little imagination to envisage how such behavior might provoke Dev; she had never doubted his utter ruthlessness, his intolerance of meddlers. What might that mean for Armand?

She had a sudden, frighteningly vivid recollection of a May night, and that strange little man stretched out on the headland, his dead eyes staring up at the stars, and of Devereux standing over him, knife in hand. . . . The man had never been found. It was as though he had never been. She supposed that Jason must have taken the body out to sea.

Nom de Dieu! No . . . no, he would not! Not with Armand!

She jumped violently as Kit's voice spoke in her ear. "You are very pensive of a sudden, my fine gallant— after all your gaiety!" He was peering intently down at her through the slit in his mask. "Is it the disapproval of neighbors, or are you worrying about that young rip of a brother?"

For a moment Madalena was tempted to blurt out her fears, but how could she do so without revealing too much? She was beginning to doubt her capacity for intrigue; to lie to Kit would be a shabby thing, not worthy of him . . . and besides, he had, at times, an uncanny perception.

She said overbrightly, "Armand is very silly, I think, to be missing all this."

"And not like him, would you say?" Kit queried gently. "But then, he has not been himself these past few days. You must have noticed it for yourself, had you not been so . . . preoccupied."

Guilty color flooded her face. "Kit . . ."

"It's all right, my dear. I don't mean to spoil your evening." Kit took her arm and led her firmly toward the dance. "But I must warn you, Maddie, that tomorrow I mean to know the whole of it, so don't think to hide away from me."

Hide away! But of course—Devereux's secret room! That is where Armand must be! Madalena smiled brilliantly up at Kit in her relief, and longed for the music to end.

No one saw her slip away. Soon she was running between hedgerows already crusted with a heavy hoarfrost. The whole landscape shimmered under the clear, hard brilliance of a three-quarter moon.

Madalena hugged Armand's cloak tight about her as she ran, half-stumbling along tracks hard-rutted and made treacherous by ice. Her thin pumps and silk stockings afforded scant protection, but she was intent only on reaching the manor and scarcely noticed the discomfort.

The lower windows of Lytten Manor were ablaze with lights, but there was no sound to disturb the vast stillness of the night. She crept with extreme caution past each one, and had almost gained the library when a stone skidded from beneath her foot. It ricocheted across the frozen ground with the force of an exploding bullet. Madalena crouched, the blood drumming in her ears, until all was silence again. *"Doucement, imbécile!"* she admonished herself with severity. "Of what use are you to Armand if you are discovered?"

It had not occurred to her until that moment that the library windows might have been made fast after her previous night excursion, but thankfully the latch gave under her hand. Stepping inside the empty room, she made her way soundlessly across to the study. There, her spirits plummeted, for the paneling showed a gaping hole, and the secret chamber appeared to be empty. She approached it with lagging steps and then was drawn inside by a curious smell of musty dampness. Set in the floor behind the paneling, a square black hole gaped, stimulating Madalena's already overstretched imagination. "An oubliette! Ah, my poor Armand!"

She rushed forward and sank to her knees. Almost at once she saw the steps, and with the flood of relief came the voices, echoing up from below and growing fainter even as she listened. A secret passage, *enfin!* Insatiable curiosity pushed all thoughts of Armand from her mind, and she began to scramble down the steps, down and down, with the cold striking deep into her bones as the rough-hewn stones became slimy, so that she almost lost her footing.

At the bottom, a passage had been gouged out of the cliffside, cutting a tortuous path ahead of her. She hugged the wall, inching her way forward, following the voices and the weird half-shadows cast by a bobbing lantern somewhere ahead of her. Soon the voices began to sound nearer, and turning a corner, she saw, not far ahead of her, two men, one of them Devereux's man Jason. Between them they carried something—a long, unwieldy something, wrapped around with cloth and tied!

Madalena's heart gave a sickening jolt, all her fears for Armand rushing back. *Sacré Nom!* Was he, after all, to be quietly disposed of, as had that other poor man?

She hastened her step and gradually became conscious of a freshening in the air. The passage turned sharply and widened, and straight ahead, etched against the moonlight, the *Seamew* rode gently on her mooring ropes close up to the jetty.

The two men heaved their burden over the side, where it landed on the deck with a sickening thud. Then they climbed aboard and disappeared.

Madalena had no idea how long she stood, her thoughts struggling for coherence. Almost at once, it seemed, the men were stepping ashore again. She pressed back into a fissure in the rock face, her arms wrapped tight about her shuddering frame and her jaw clamped on chattering teeth.

They passed so close that Jason's heavy greatcoat brushed her legs, its pungent odor of brine catching at her throat. His slow, gruff voice boomed in her ear.

". . . told 'im straight, I didn't like it—getting mixed up with them frogs. But you know 'is grace—pig-headed and arrogant, like his father afore him. 'E'll press 'is luck once too often, mark my words . . . and so I told 'im . . ."

The rest was lost in the echoing vaults of the passage. When the last sound had died away, Madalena came stiffly from her hiding place.

Aboard the boat, she stood listening for the least suggestion of movement; there was none, save the sibilant smack of the tide against the *Seamew*'s side. The brightness of the night illuminated the deck. It was empty. So that meant she must go below. The cavernous mouth of the companionway did not invite entry, and as she descended, the utter futility of trying to search without any light became apparent, for at each step the blackness became more complete. On the lower deck she stood, her back hairs prickling, took a few tentative steps—and banged her shin.

Peste! An exploratory hand closed on what seemed to be a kind of table or desk. *"Sot!"* she addressed it crossly. "Why are you placed so that one must fall over you?"

She felt her way along the table, and as her eyes grew accustomed to the darkness, she saw that small windows ran along either side of the cabin, and from the light filtering through, she was presently able to discern vague outlines—two sleeping berths, the table with which she had collided, and, at the far end, a dark mass that could be cupboards or an extra compartment. But there was nothing resembling the bundle she had seen.

"Armand," she called softly. *"Chéri—*make me some sign if you are here. I do not know if we have much time!"

Nothing answered her. Not a sound. And the fear that had been pushed to the back of her mind would be denied no longer—the fear that Armand was already dead and beyond her help. Yet she still continued drearily to search.

The sound, when it came, was from above her. *Sacré mille diables!* The men were back! Madalena felt her way, stumbling, to the far end of the cabin, and found a cupboard behind which she could crouch. For what seemed an age, the feet tramped above her. Several times the boat lurched alarmingly and she was almost dislodged. Of a surety, the weather must be growing rough!

And then, as the motion became more regular, it dawned upon her with growing dismay that it was not the weather that had changed, but the boat. The *Seamew* was putting out to sea!

Chapter 12

THE BOAT WAS NO longer moving. Madalena had not been sure at first. Still huddled in her corner, she had alternately dozed and fought against attacks of cramp until time had ceased to have any meaning. She had no idea where she was—or what was to become of her; she was tired and cross and just a little frightened. Back in Lytten Tracy, all would be in uproar, and Tante Esmé would be prostrate with a spasm! No, decidedly it was better not to think of Lytten Tracy.

One thing was certain; Dev was on board. He had come down to the cabin earlier carrying a lantern. She had watched him hang the lantern from a hook and stand for a few minutes reading at the table. As he read, he had unwrapped a package to disclose a quantity of succulent-looking ham and chicken, together with some thick crusty bread.

Madalena, by now ravenously hungry, had been obliged to watch as he consumed the best part of it before her outraged eyes. Almost she was tempted to reveal herself to him there and then; only the certainty of his rage deterred her. Perhaps there would yet be some way to evade his wrath—if he would just leave some of the food. . . .

But in the end he had left the cabin, taking the remainder of the package with him, and Madalena was forced to subdue her grumbling stomach, for a swift search of the cabin revealed not so much as a crumb remaining.

But at least he had left the lantern, and she was no longer obliged to endure the darkness. When she was sure the boat had stopped moving, she again stirred her stiff limbs in order to peer cautiously out one of the windows. It was dark, and she could make nothing of the outside.

"Voyons," she muttered. "This begins to be difficult. One has not found Armand, who is very likely dead or concealed elsewhere—and now it seems we have arrived! But where do we arrive? In France, perhaps?"

The thought stirred her blood a little; she strove again to make something of the view, but there was only the obscurity of a sky from which moon and stars had vanished, and some kind of blacker bulk near at hand, a cliff, perhaps. And if a cliff, then there would be a beach.

As if to confirm this supposition, two shadowy figures crossed her line of vision, reached the side of the boat, and leaped nimbly ashore, and there came a crunching of feet on pebbles.

Their imminent departure galvanized Madalena into instant activity; if Dev and Jason were both to leave the boat, one would be left alone! Even the prospect of Dev's inevitable wrath paled before the more dreadful prospect of being abandoned in so godforsaken a spot!

She had just reached the deck when a series of explosions shattered the silent blackness, followed by much indistinct shouting. She swallowed on the scream that rose in her throat, and grasped the rail, straining to pierce the gloom. She thought she could make out several figures struggling on the ground, and even as she waited, there came a further single shot. It seemed to release her.

Her feet flew across the shingle, her incoherent supplications to the *bon Dieu* alternately entreating and demanding of Him that Dev should be spared, so that she did not see the body in time and sprawled her length across it. Fighting down panic, she forced herself to look closer. The man was a stranger, and he was quite unmistakably dead!

She turned abruptly away, and found Jason lying close by, a pistol in his hand. At first she thought he, too, was dead; there was a fearful gash on the side of his head. Madalena pushed a hand inside his coat; his heart was beating—very faintly, but at least he lived!

So! She drew a sobbing breath. Then Dev must be one of the men still fighting. She came upon them quite suddenly. There had been two assailants, but one now lay motionless; the other was locked with Dev in a deadly grip, and in one hand she could see the gleam of a knife blade.

Madalena's eyes blazed as she circled them, seeking for some way to help. Her voice was locked in her throat. To her inexperienced eye the stranger seemed to be the stronger; Dev was being borne slowly backward, and though his grip was on the wrist that held the knife, he could not wrest it from the man's grasp.

"Sainte Vierge!" she prayed in her despair. "Aid me! There must be some way for me . . ." Her glance fell again on the dead man, and from him to where something lay discarded among the pebbles—something that gleamed!

She snatched up the knife and sought to plunge it into the back of Dev's assailant; it would not penetrate the thick greatcoat! In despair she renewed her efforts, but her strength was not enough. They were on the ground now. Soon it would be too late! She heard the sound of her own sobbing, as the man arched back to deliver his coup de grace, exposing for an instant the bareness of his neck. Without hesitation she plunged the knife in with all her strength, and felt the sickening jar run up her arm as the hilt hit his collarbone. His scream died instantly to a gurgle, and he fell backward, with blood spurting from his neck.

Madalena would not let herself look at him. She turned instead to Devereux. He lay, supported on one hand, gasping for air and fighting dizziness. Madalena waited anxiously.

The sky was beginning to pale slightly, and in the cold wash of light from the sea, she discerned something dark dripping and spreading on the shingle beneath him.

"Dev! You are hurt!"

He raised his head, shaking it as if he would clear the mists from his eyes. He seemed unsurprised to see her —in fact, Madalena very much doubted if he was even aware who she was.

"Damned pistol ball . . . left shoulder . . ." he muttered thickly. "Get Jason."

There was a cold sickness in her stomach, but she made herself be calm. "Jason is hit on the head and is quite unconscious, *chéri,* so we must manage without him."

Devereux swore and struggled to rise. "Can't stay here . . . bleeding like a pig . . . must get back . . . to the boat."

"Yes, of course we will go to the boat, *mon pauvre;* it will be much the best place for you to be." Madalena's voice was shaking; she could not prevent it, but he was too preoccupied to notice. *"Voyons,* I will place your good arm around my shoulder—so—and you may lean on me as much as you wish."

He came uncertainly to his feet, and Madalena staggered under his weight. "That is splendid!" she urged breathlessly. "And now, hold tightly to me and be tranquil —we shall soon arrive!"

Together they traced an erratic path back along the beach. Getting Dev onto the boat was incredibly difficult, and he half-stumbled, half-fell down the companionway into the cabin, where, thankfully, the lamp still burned. There he collapsed, ashen-faced with exhaustion.

In his pocket she discovered a brandy flask and made him drink. When he presently hauled himself into a sitting position, he looked only a little less gray.

"Now," he gasped, "if I might . . . trouble you to assist me . . . I'll rid myself of this accursed coat . . . view the damage."

Madalena threw off her own cloak and set to work with fingers that were stupid and clumsy. When greatcoat and then coat were finally stripped off, they both stared in silence at the rent shirt. The bullet, fired at close range, should have passed through him, but the thickness of the greatcoat had impeded its progress, and it had been driven in fairly high up, between arm and collarbone, dragging the edges of the shirt with it.

Madalena knew that he must already have lost a great deal too much blood in the course of that dreadful fight —and now, with the exertions of the last few minutes, the blood was again pumping forth steadily. It needed a doctor, and she had no idea where one might be found.

She scanned the cabin. "Bandages. Dev, I must make a pad to stanch the blood!"

"Shirts," he muttered, leaning back with closed eyes. "Bottom drawer . . . cupboard . . ."

She found them at last and threw them onto the bunk —beautiful shirts of the finest lawn, which she tore recklessly and tore again until she had made a thick pad and completed the seemingly impossible task of securing it tightly.

Only then did she relax—and found she was shaking. The brandy flask was pushed into her hand, and she gulped at it gratefully.

Dev's glance was resting upon her, frowning. ". . . don't understand . . . why you are here."

Madalena made herself very busy. "Oh, it is a very long story, and not of importance at this moment. Dev, what are we to do? You are very much in need of a doctor!"

"Not a chance, little one. I doubt there is a doctor within twenty miles."

"But the bullet?"

"Must assuredly come out. Old Jason will . . ."

"*Chéri*, I told you . . ."

He moved his head wearily. "Oh, yes, the bump on the head. . . . Well, he's a wiry old bird—should be back in his senses by now. If you will oblige me by rousing him, Jason will dig it out in a trice."

Madalena looked horrified. Devereux's smile was meant to be reassuring. "It won't be the first time Jason has dug lead out of me, child. He's reckoned something of an expert!"

She flared with a sudden anger that was tinged with terror. "Oh, I am out of all patience! And I will tell you, that you are all the same—you men! Like small boys playing dangerous games!" Her voice became choked. "And one day you will be sorry, for I will not be here to help!"

She ran from the cabin, tears blinding her, not hearing her name called, not seeing the outstretched hand.

In a short time she was back. Her steps were dragging, and the tears were drying on her white, frightened face.

"Jason will not respond. I have shouted, and I have shaken him, but he lies like one dead."

"Maybe he is . . . dead."

"No," she said quickly. "His pulse still beats, but very fast, and . . . and not good. And the bump on his head is very bad!"

"I . . . see." Dev closed his eyes again. His body seemed to sag, and Madalena, her anger forgotten, went to his side and put her hand in his.

"I am sorry," she said inadequately.

His fingers returned her pressure. "Poor infant," he murmured. "I would not willingly have had you dragged into this . . . and yet"—he sighed—"and yet, God help me, I am glad to have you here!"

His eyes opened suddenly, and he looked straight at her. "Why *are* you here?"

Madalena fidgeted uneasily and then told him.

The satanic eyebrows quivered. "Dear me—what a villain you have made of me! First a traitor . . . and now a murderer!"

"Ma foi! That is unjust! What am I to suppose when you shroud all you do in mystery?"

He frowned. "But do you really see me dispatching Armand in so cavalier a fashion?"

"I . . . I have tried not to think it, but I am not blind to your nature, and . . . and if Armand endangered your plans . . ." Her voice sank to a whisper. "I think perhaps you might . . ."

"So! I make you my compliments. Your reading of my character is masterly and . . . illuminating!" The words were jerked out, and the twist of his lips, the very sarcasm of the words, betrayed how she had hurt him.

"You see," she explained miserably, "I cannot help remembering the man on the cliff . . . and . . . and I did see Jason and the other one carrying something to the boat."

"Spare sail sheets?" he suggested tersely.

"Oh." Madalena considered the possibility. "Then if it was not Armand, where is he, pray? For I will not believe that you do not have a hand in his disappearance!"

Devereux leaned back and sighed wearily. "I trust that by now he is in London with Lady Serena, who will assist him in laying information against Daniel Merchent."

The amber eyes grew wide. "Lady Serena . . . Daniel? Oh, but I do not understand! Is Daniel to be arrested?"

"Do you mind if we defer explanations until later?" A thin smile touched the lips compressed with pain. "However, to set that bloodthirsty mind of yours at rest—the man on the cliff was working for me . . . Merchent killed him . . ." His voice was beginning to fade.

Madalena made him lie down, for it was obvious that so much talking had taken all his strength. She would think later.

"You have lost a great deal too much blood," she said distractedly.

"Must get rid of this accursed bullet," he muttered. "I have a twenty-mile ride ahead of me."

"Dieu! How can you talk of riding in such a state!"

"I must." His eyes glazed and cleared. He grasped her hand with sudden urgency. "You will have to remove the bullet."

Madalena was shocked into immobility. "That is a monstrous suggestion!" she gasped. "You are delirious even to think it!"

"No—I promise you. It is not so difficult a task. It needs only a steady hand and a degree of concentration."

"No!"

He drew a steadying breath. "Is it the blood?" he queried harshly. "Are you squeamish?"

Madalena snatched her hand away. Her eyes blazed. "No—oh, how can you think me so poor a creature! It is"—her voice faltered—"it is that I might kill you!"

His breath caught on a wild laugh. "And if you do not make the attempt, this lump of lead will certainly kill me. I was ever a gambler, infant, and I prefer to take my chance with you."

Panic gripped her. "Perhaps Jason will recover."

"And if he does not . . . or if he is too late?"

He was right, and she knew it, but even so . . . "You do not know what it is you ask," she whispered.

"Yes I do." His voice was beginning to sound unbearably strained. "Come here and look at me, *mignonne.*"

She met his eyes, now luminous with pain, but steady. "I had not told you, but I had made certain arrangements for your father. . . ." She stiffened. "His safety *may* depend upon my recovery, so I am asking you to trust yourself . . . as I trust you!"

After a moment she nodded, unable to speak, but flinched as he went on, "Should things go badly for me

. . . and Jason, I cannot direct you . . . stay with the boat. Someone will come."

"You are talking too much!" Madalena complained fiercely.

"I've almost finished," he rasped. "Now, you will find a special small knife in the top drawer of that cabinet . . . and in the cupboard, a bottle of brandy."

Madalena laid everything ready that she would need, made all her preparations in an orderly fashion. She poured brandy over the knife blade as Dev instructed her, but her hand shook so much that she spilled it.

"Easy with that bottle!" He rescued it from her trembling fingers and drank deeply. "Now, when you are ready . . ."

She raised the knife, and her agonized glance flew to his face. "I . . . cannot!"

"For God's sake, Madalena!" The brandy was slurring his voice; it loosed also a groan of pure despair. "This way, I have a chance. Do you want me to die of a poisoned wound?"

Her breath caught on a shocked sob. "Pardon, *chéri*, I am now quite ready . . . and you will not die at all, I promise you."

What followed was to remain with Madalena ever after as a hideous nightmare. She deliberately emptied her mind of everything but what she must do; her jaw was clamped tight with concentration. The light from the lamp was not good, but it mattered little, since she could see nothing but the blood that welled up faster than she could wipe it away.

Her nerves were stretched as steel grated against bone for the second time in a matter of hours, but with grim determination she continued her careful probe. When the tip of the knife found the bullet, she could hardly believe it.

"Get the . . . blade . . . underneath." Devereux

ground the words out, still unbelievably conscious. "Lever
. . . gently."

The first time, it skidded away, and she cursed it, sobbing.

"Easy," he gasped.

The palm of her hand was slippery with sweat. She rubbed it on her breeches and took a fresh grip. This time, very slowly, the bullet began to move, and suddenly it slithered out, splattering her with blood, and rolled on the floor at her feet.

In the same instant she felt Dev sag under her hand, and terror rose in her throat. But he had simply swooned away. Working with feverish haste, she swabbed away as much of the blood as she could, and taking the bottle from his limp hand, poured brandy recklessly into the wound; only the *bon Dieu* knew if it would help, but one hoped. She tied the final strip of bandage into place, and was aware quite suddenly that, in spite of the cold, sweat was running down her face and sticking the shirt to her aching shoulders.

Her trembling legs carried her as far as the deck. There, the cold air hit her lungs and sent her crawling to the rail, where she retched violently again and again, until she leaned her head against the rail at last, exhausted and shivering.

It was daylight now, but a mist had descended, enveloping all. There was no sound in the world beyond the cold slap of the surf, and somewhere, the mournful cry of a solitary gull.

Madalena wondered about Jason; he would assuredly die of the cold out there. She brought blankets from the spare bunk and managed to drag him into the shelter of an overhanging rock before wrapping the blankets around him. His pulse seemed stronger, but he did not stir.

Back in the cabin, the air reeked of brandy and congealing blood. Dev's breathing was noisy and fitful. Madalena pushed the tousled hair from his face, touching the silver wings that lent him so much distinction. In repose, the pale features lost much of their cynicism, and he looked oddly defenseless.

She covered him with an extra blanket, and then, pulling one about her own shoulders, she sank to her knees, her head resting beside him on the bunk. She cried a little, and she prayed a lot—and then she must have slept, for she awoke to fingers moving in her hair, and a voice, weak, but blessedly sardonic.

"What's this, my Madalena? On your knees for me, like your little Madonna. Am I not past praying for?"

Slowly she lifted her head. Dev's eyes were fever-bright, and the fingers that brushed her cheek burned hot and dry.

"Madonnas should not have tear-ravaged faces," he murmured.

With a sob, she buried her face in his hand, and fresh tears flowed. "I am s-sorry, but I am so happy!" she stammered in confusion. "I had so great a fear that I might kill you."

"Devil a bit," he protested feebly. "If you will return my brandy to me, I shall do very well."

Madalena scrambled to her feet. She observed the two bright patches of color in his cheeks. "I think more brandy will not help you now," she said uncertainly. "It will enrich too much the blood."

"Good," he snapped, with some of the old arrogance. "I like my blood rich. Don't be officious, child—my brandy, if you please."

But she shook her head resolutely and found him some cordial, which he took with an ill grace. As the morning wore on, his fever mounted. Periods of awareness alternated with bouts of delirium, and Madalena watched with increasing anxiety; a doctor would doubtless recommend that he should be bled, but *Dieu!* Had he not bled enough?

Once, his eyes focused on her like red-hot coals.

"Damned stupid—this," he muttered, shivering. "Never happened before."

Madalena piled another blanket on him, tucking it in so that he could not throw it off. "It is the fever, *mon amour*—it will pass," she reassured him, but he was already rambling again.

She decided quite suddenly that she must at least try to find a doctor.

Outside, the mist had finally drifted away, but it was a gray day, with flurries of snow in the wind. The boat was safely berthed in a tiny inlet screened by the rocks, which should safeguard it from the prying eyes of anyone foolhardy enough to approach the beach on such a day.

Madalena stopped briefly to look at Jason. His pulse was undoubtedly growing stronger; with luck he might soon recover his senses, and Dev would not be alone.

She fastened her cloak tightly about her and turned, a small, rather forlorn figure, plodding with great determination up the beach.

She found a farmhouse, but when repeated banging on the door produced no results, she walked around to the rear of the building and found a gray gelding tethered in its stall.

"*Bonjour,* my friend," she greeted him. "You do not appear to have an owner, so I believe I must borrow you without permission."

Here, a difficulty presented itself. "For it is impossible for me to put that great heavy saddle on you," she told him, and the placid animal whinnied agreement. "Assuredly, it is many years since I rode bareback, but one must contrive!"

She found the bridle, and with much stretching and tugging, she fitted it on, talking all the while to the horse. "And now I must mount you, and I do not at all see how I am to do so."

Some kind of mounting block was required. There were

signs that the stables were used for storage, and a thorough search unearthed a lone half-anker of brandy. "The very thing. Doubtless you are contraband!"

She found the squat barrel not tall enough, but the sides of the stall were of slatted wood sufficient to support her tiny foot, and after several abortive attempts and many Gallic epithets, she sat triumphantly astride the horse's back. "Bon! And now, my friend—*en avant!*"

Chapter 13

A SUDDEN, SPUME-LADEN squall snatched at Madalena's cloak and lifted it high. She roused from a weary stupor to clutch its folds close again. She straightened her aching back and yawned. *Dieu merci*—they were not lost, as she had feared, for here at last was the track to the beach.

She had been riding forever, it seemed, and with nothing to show. Dev had been right; there was no doctor to be found. She had asked at . . . oh, so many doors—to be met for the most part with apathy, sometimes with downright hostility, from dispirited women whose own men had long since been lost to them and who therefore cared nothing for the plight of a stranger.

Only one poor, wandering soul had invited her into a tiny, pitifully bare kitchen and had insisted that Madalena should take a bowl of hot, watery broth. She had rambled on unceasingly on all manner of topics, but on the subject of doctors she had been persistently vague. And for Madalena, whose *derrière* had long since lost all sensation, and for whom the descent from the horse and the greater difficulty of remounting had been a painful experience, the hospitality had been more frustrating than comforting.

The gusty wind was chasing ominous black clouds across the moon. Its biting edge began to clear her brain, and she wondered how she would find Dev. One hoped that he had not thrown off his blankets and taken a chill. She supposed that it must be close on midnight, for the horse had grown tired and had taken his time. At last he turned, of his own volition, into the cobbled yard—and stopped.

And then, without quite knowing why, Madalena felt the back hairs lift on her scalp.

From close by there came a scraping sound, and a torch was set aflame—and then another, and another, until she was encircled by blazing flambeaux, trailing their smoke into the wind.

In the silence, her heart seemed to be hammering against her ribs; she searched the shadows beyond the flames to the still faces, etched like masks, with no vestige of humanity.

Her glance came to rest on a giant of a man who held no torch—a flamboyant, swaggering figure dressed in a ragbag of assorted finery. A fine embroidered waistcoat gleamed in the light, straining over the beginning of a paunch. His head thrust forward, bull-necked, from massive shoulders, and—*Dieu me sauve!* Madalena mentally crossed herself—what a head! All black hair and whiskers! One arm was flung in genial fashion about the shoulders of a young boy, and while his bright black eyes looked her over, he unhurriedly winkled his teeth with a fine gold-and-ivory toothpick. This he finally stabbed in Madalena's direction.

"This is the one, Jean Paul? You are sure?"

There was excited, stumbling affirmation from the boy. "It is him—I swear it! He was with the *anglais* when they murdered Philippe and Guidal. I saw him as plain as now. . . . One cannot mistake that hair. . . . And I saw him again when he took Brutus from the stable."

There was a muttering among the men. The circle closed tighter, so that the acrid fumes from the torches caught at her throat and made her eyes smart.

"And now he rides in again, my friends. And Le Loup-garou wonders, now—does the *anglais* come again from the sea, heh?"

These last words were flung at Madalena.

"No," she gasped.

"I think we go down to see for ourselves. Already I have lost four men."

He can't even count, thought Madalena in disgust—and stopped herself just in time from saying so. To admit any knowledge of the men on the beach was to admit that she knew how they had died.

She was dragged from the horse, stiff-legged and with every muscle quivering, and with a musket barrel in her ribs she was prodded down the track to the beach.

Ahead of her, the gross man who called himself Le Loup-garou—the werewolf—had stopped. The bodies of the two men were lying where she and Dev had left them; she watched him lift the first callously with the toe of his boot and roll it face up; he grunted and repeated the process with the other. It seemed to her a strangely callous way to treat a friend—and why had they been left here all this time?

The big man tossed a clove of garlic into his mouth and chewed noisily before looking up.

"You know this scum, any of you? No?"

Madalena was now more bewildered than ever; her tired brain could make no sense of it. If these were not Philippe and Guidal, then who were they? A sharp dig in the ribs propelled her forward again. Soon the other body would be found, and Jason also, if he was not recovered . . . and then the *Seamew* would come into view. She could think of no way to turn these men aside.

And then panic, so far contained, swept over her in frightening waves. The little anchorage was now visible, but Jason had gone, and of the *Seamew* there was no trace! It was as if she had never been!

Back at the farmhouse, the door was pushed wide, and Madalena was sent stumbling, to measure her length on the uneven flags. She lay fighting for the return of her breath, while feet tramped and shuffled around and over her. Lamps were being lit, and a fire was started in the huge cavern of a grate.

In the darkness and the dust there were other scufflings, too; something ran across her hair, and she bit back a scream. To distract her thoughts from this new terror, she fell to considering the exigencies of her situation. Men had been left to watch on the beach, so sure were these brigands that the *anglais* would come. But she knew differently.

Dev had gone, and since she utterly rejected the possibility that he would abandon her, she must suppose that Jason had discovered him, still insensible, and had sailed at once for home. The thought that he might perhaps be dead lay as a stone against her heart.

So she was alone. The knowledge chilled her, for certainly these men were of a breed quite without mercy.

As if to confirm her fears, she was presently hauled to her feet by a squat gorilla of a man, who bent her arm agonizingly behind her back. With her free hand she attempted to brush away some of the dust and cobwebs that clung to her face and clothes, a display of fastidiousness much enjoyed by those who pressed around her. The close proximity of so many unwashed bodies made her feel sick.

They were in a kitchen, of sorts—scantily furnished and obviously used by these men from time to time. Two badly smoking lamps hung from hooks along a beam; in the center of the room and gracing a rough-hewn table, an eight-branch solid silver candelabrum glowed with incongruous beauty, flanked by an earthenware flagon of wine and a stick of bread and some cheese.

Here, the big man spread himself in the only reasonable chair, directing operations. Now and again he speared a hunk of cheese on the end of a wicked-looking stiletto, and as he chewed, he watched the antics of Jean Paul, who had relieved Madalena of her splendid cloak and now swaggered before them all, twirling its folds.

"Enough!" he growled at last. "Now, then, pretty boy, we will have some answers."

"*Stupide!*" she retorted. "I will tell you nothing."

She heard the hiss of his drawn breath.

"The pup needs a lesson in manners," grunted a harsh voice. "Perhaps he would then respect his elders."

Indignation momentarily swamped every other emotion in Madalena's breast. "*Ma foi!* Should I respect such as you—who are ignorant and uncouth and live like pigs! And if we are to talk of manners . . ." This injudicious catalog of their shortcomings ended on a gasp, as her arm was given a vicious twist.

The brigand's whiskers twitched petulantly, and his voice grew soft. "You think old Loup-garou stupid, heh? You are not the first to make such an error." The blade of his stiletto slid beneath her chin, its touch like silk. "Now, you listen, my fine brave friend—and you listen good. If I want answers, you will give me answers. And no little mistakes—understand? Because Frochot here has a very keen ear, and he would not like it."

The face of the gorilla loomed hopefully at her shoulder, and Madalena knew despair. The knife was removed, and she breathed.

"Your name, boy?"

"Armand," she lied, stammering in spite of herself.

"Good—that is good! And now, Armand, you will tell me, when do you expect the *anglais,* and what is his business here?"

She was silent, thinking suddenly of her papa; would he still get to safety now that Dev was gone?

On a signal, the hold on her arm tightened another notch, and pain, like red-hot needles, shot up into her shoulders. The brigand chief watched her reactions with interest; almost casually he began to pare his nails with the stiletto, pausing once to drink copiously from the flagon of wine.

Madalena was conscious of a growing air of expectancy among the men. When the silence had stretched her nerve endings to their limit, Le Loup-garou looked up, his pig eyes bright, as though he had thought of one big joke.

"I think perhaps you do not understand your situation so good, little bantam—it is even possible that you do not know us. . . ." His tone indicated how great was her misfortune. "There is a name they give to us in these parts—*chauffeurs.*"

Her look of horror appeared to gratify him. "Ah, you are quick! Good—it saves much tedious explanation. But until now you have perhaps not given credit to the rumors which abound, heh?"

He smiled, and a sweat of pure terror washed over Madalena.

"Now, I ask you one more time—the *anglais?*"

"I cannot tell you what I do not know," she insisted desperately.

The big man sighed. "Oh, you *will* tell me, boy. In a very short time you will be babbling like an idiot, begging me to listen! Did I not explain how Frochot here is a genius . . . an artist!" He kissed his fingertips. "Why, he can make people remember things they did not even know they knew!"

The men were growing tired of all the talk.

"The fire is good and hot. . . ."

"Fry him a little, Frochot, old son. Then we shall hear what tune our bird will sing."

She was dragged, protesting, toward the fierce heat of

the fire. For good measure her arm was given a final vicious wrench, which almost lifted her off her feet and brought a strangled scream to her throat. The red-hot needles stabbed, radiated in waves across her back; they tore at the delicate tissues of her breast so that involuntarily she arched her back in an effort to ease the pressure—and made it worse.

Through the mists and the roaring in her ears there was a shout. The big man was so close that the garlic on his breath suffocated her. The long, slim blade of his knife pointed straight at her stomach.

Madalena found herself watching him with a kind of detached fascination. "So! Does he then mean to kill me now—quickly? He does not look so merciful!" In a quiet corner of her mind, time stretched into infinity. If Dev were alive and came back, would he ever know what became of her? And Papa—she prayed that the *bon Dieu* would keep him safe. And Armand also. She thought of the good people in England. Perhaps they would miss her a little. . . .

"Why does the great oaf stare so? Perhaps if I taunt him again he will lose his temper and stick his knife in me. . . . It is not much of a choice, *enfin,* but I do not think I can be brave if they do that other barbaric thing! *Peste!* The fool is grinning again—that is not good. He is mad, I think, but dangerous. . . ."

The stiletto snaked upward with terrifying suddenness, and Madalena screamed. There was a rending sound, and the crimson cord of her jerkin and the shirt beneath it were sliced through.

The brigand stood back, laughing uproariously, enjoying the spectacle of Madalena endeavoring, one-handed, to clutch the torn edges of her shirt across her budding breasts.

"Here is a turn of events, *mes amis!* Our pugnacious little bantam cock is a *poseur!* Release the mademoiselle at once, Frochot—can you not see how she is desperate to cover her embarrassment!"

Still he chortled, but his eyes made Madalena go hot and then very cold. Deep down, this, more than anything, was what she had been dreading. Coarse hands with indescribably dirty fingernails pawed her, grabbed at her shirt as she fought to keep it closed; her ears rang with obscenities, and a harsh voice, rising above the rest to remark that they had never before fried a girl, was drowned out by other quite specific and horrifying predictions of her final fate.

"Gentlemen! Please! You are frightening our guest!" The big man was in high good humor. He sketched a travesty of a courtly bow. "Mademoiselle, forgive their overenthusiasm, I beg you! They grow greedy, like children suddenly faced with a surfeit of sweetmeats. And do you know why, heh?"

Madalena feared this affable mood more than all the bombast; she awaited his next words with a sense of dread.

He leaned forward confidentially. "It is the breeches, you understand? To see such a nice young mademoiselle in breeches gives them quite false notions . . . so I think we have them off, heh?"

There was much laughter, and the rabble moved closer. A sudden draft set the flames leaping, but Madalena, in a paroxysm of shivering, felt neither the heat nor the cold.

And then a voice she had thought never to hear again was threatening with cold fury, "Just move so much as one muscle, you old devil, and you get my bullet right between your lecherous eyes!"

Madalena turned on a sob, to see Devereux striding across the room, a pistol leveled unerringly at Le Loup-garou. She hastily pulled her clothes together, ashamed that he should see her so in front of this *canaille*.

Dev looked very pale and drawn; someone had fashioned a sling for his arm from a cravat, and he wore his greatcoat slung across his shoulders. She wanted very much to fling herself on his chest, but to do so would impede his aim, so she stared mutely, her eyes wide against her tears.

"There was a scream," he said abruptly. "Are you all right, *mignonne?*"

She nodded, and he turned on the brigand chief with searing vehemence. "If you have harmed her in any way, you misbegotten savage, I will personally cut your miserable heart into little pieces and feed it to the fishes!"

The other shifted awkwardly. "Easy, *mon vieux*. I give you my word there was no more than a little gentle interrogation." As Devereux's glance moved to take in the state of Madalena's clothes, he added with a nervous laugh, "Ah, well—how was I to know that she was your woman?"

Madalena stared, uncomprehending. This was not a conversation between strangers; rather, there was a kind of rough camaraderie. It was very odd. And then Dev had put away his pistol and was reaching out for her. She flew to his side, and his arm closed tight about her; it was like being in paradise.

Above her head the arguments and explanations continued; it was made clear to her that Dev was not the enemy of these men—that Daniel Merchent was the *anglais* they were seeking. He had killed their compatriots, and Armand had been with him, which was why they had mistaken her. But it did not matter. Nothing mattered to her save that she had been given back that which she had thought lost forever.

Presently she became aware that Dev's arm had tightened; she felt him sway a little.

"A chair," she demanded, and when the astonished brigands stared, she rounded on them like a small fury. "Dolts! *Imbéciles!* Can you not see that monseigneur is injured and is still far from strong?"

The best armchair was dragged forward, and Devereux sank into it without a word. He was very white about the mouth. Le Loup-garou went at once to a cupboard and returned with a bottle of Armagnac and glasses. He also called two of the men aside and gave them orders, after which they silently slipped from the room.

With the Armagnac, some of Devereux's color returned, but Madalena stayed very close beside the chair, reading him a stern lecture upon the folly of attempting too much too soon. It earned little for her beyond a smile of gentle irony.

The two men returned, and some sign passed between them and their leader, who cleared his throat.

"Are you now sufficiently rested to take a few steps, *mon vieux?*"

Devereux gave him a derisive stare, and in spite of stringent protests from Madalena, came slowly to his feet.

"Do not fear, mademoiselle." The brigand grinned. "I do not seek to tire your monseigneur. In fact—quite the reverse. If you will please to follow . . ."

They were led with elaborate ceremony into an adjoining room, where flames already licked hopefully around a pile of logs in the grate; a hasty and not altogether successful attempt had been made to effect some degree of order and cleanliness.

The *pièce de résistance* of this unlikely boudoir was triumphantly displayed for their approval. It was a huge bed, of doubtful ancestry, piled with a quantity of equally dubious-looking rugs and furs.

The big man, however, saw nothing amiss. In high good humor he set a smoking lamp down upon a rickety dresser and beamed at them.

"*Voilà, mes amis!* Does old Loup-garou not provide for you a veritable love nest, heh? I tell you, in that bed you will be as snug as two ticks on a dog's back!"

From the crowded doorway came a chorus of ribald assent, interspersed with many helpful and extremely graphic suggestions, which had Madalena's cheeks burning by the time the door clicked shut.

She felt suddenly and quite ridiculously shy, until, meeting Dev's eye, her awkwardness dissolved in laughter.

As abruptly as it had come, the laughter died away. They stood looking at each other until Madalena thought that her heart would burst; then Dev's good arm was pulling her forward, crushing the breath from her body, and their lips clung as though they would never again be parted.

"You shouldn't have gone off like that, you crazy idiot!" Dev muttered, punctuating his strictures with kisses rained on her eyes, her lips, and the trembling hollow at the base of her throat. "I told you to stay with the boat."

"I thought I would get help, but there was none to be had, and when I returned, these brigands were here, and your boat had gone. I did not know what to do. . . ." Her breath caught on a sob.

"And poor old Jason had me halfway home before I came to my senses!"

"I was half-afraid that I had killed you, after all," she said fiercely, "and I too wanted to die!"

He caught her close again, and as her arms slid around his neck, her aching muscles protested.

He swore. "That old devil *has* hurt you. I'll go and break his head!"

"No . . . no—it is nothing."

"Nothing! My God—when I think what almost happened . . ."

The strain was back in his voice, and Madalena was immediately contrite.

"Come. You must lie down at once. Oh, I am a great *stupide* to keep you standing for so long."

She chivvied him into the bed and insisted on pulling off his boots. "For I am an expert," she gasped, giving a last great heave. "With a father and a brother, I had much practice." She sent him a quick look. "What about Papa, Dev? Will he be safe?"

"I believe so, child. We shall soon know for sure."

Under his sardonic gaze she piled the rugs and skins on top of him, her nose wrinkling in distaste at their musty smell. As she pushed the last rug up under his chin, his fingers closed around her wrist.

"And what about you, little one? God knows, you must be worn out. And it *is* a very large bed."

Madalena knelt, poised on the edge of the bed, her heart thudding against her ribs, her eyes enormous and smudged with fatigue.

"You must know you are safe, *mignonne*." Dev's smile was gentle, half-rueful. "In spite of that old bear's lecherous optimism, I am clearly in no state to ravish anyone tonight."

Madalena's heart had now leaped into her throat; it constricted her breath, so that her reply, when it came, was scarcely audible.

"Do you think you might contrive to manage if I promise not to struggle?"

Her words hung in the silence.

"I have shocked you."

His thumb was tracing the delicate pattern of veins in her wrist, where a pulse was beating wildly. He kept his voice very even. "No, *ma petite*—you could never shock me." He looked up to regard her intently. "But I think you have not truly considered what it is you are saying."

"Oh, but I have! And you can see that I am quite without shame!" Her chin trembled very slightly, but her eyes were ablaze with the light of her love . . . and he was lost.

"Egad! It isn't how I would have planned matters," he murmured.

"Perhaps not, *mon amour,* but this time it is I who am the seducer—and I do not think I shall be able to bear it if you reject me!"

Devereux's fingers moved slowly up into the curls at the nape of her neck, and a tremor ran through her. "You are . . . that sure, *mignonne?*"

"Oh, yes."

Yet when he would have drawn her down beside him, she resisted. "I must blow out the lamp."

"To the devil with the lamp!" murmured Dev succinctly.

Chapter 14

IT WAS GROWING light when Madalena wakened. She lay quite still, savoring a wondrous sensation of well-being. As memory flooded in, she turned eagerly, but the place at her side was empty. There was a moment of panic, and then she saw Dev outlined against the window.

He heard her, and came to sit beside her on the bed, kissing the glowing face she lifted to him.

"Little sluggard!" he teased. "No need to ask if you slept."

"Ummm." She uttered a blissful sigh and stretched with an unselfconsciously sensuous abandon which entranced him, the more so when it was suddenly transformed into a wriggle of indignation. "*Ma foi!* This bed has bugs!"

"A veritable army of them, I shouldn't wonder," he agreed.

"Oh well!" She shrugged, and grinned. "It makes no matter. What of you, *chéri?* How is your poor shoulder? Are you feeling more rested?"

"Rested? I'm not sure." He eyed her quizzically. "Did I only dream that I was bewitched by an adorable, wanton enchantress who came to my bed and wooed me with soft words?"

Madalena gurgled with delight. "It was no dream. Have you any regrets, *mon amour?*"

The question was quite without artifice; indeed, there was no need to dissemble—the totality of her love both exhilarated and distressed him. He wanted to tell her that he wasn't worth it, but her eyes, which had been heavy with sleep, now shone as though she had taken them out and polished them to a new brilliance.

He groaned. "God knows, I should regret it!"

Madalena reached up and cupped his face in her hands, drawing him down to smooth away his frown. "But you know that you do not."

He turned his face convulsively into the warm curve of her neck. Slowly, caressingly, his lips moved down over her throat, to bury themselves in the hollow of her breasts, from whence his voice rose huskily. "Would you have me prove it to you again, dearest witch?"

He felt soft laughter ripple through her; the fingers stroking the back of his neck tightened, "Oh, my Dev! How I do love you!"

Dear God! This was no way to act. He had meant to be so circumspect—an admittedly unfamiliar role for him —and to court her in conventional fashion, with the approval of her father.

He prised her hands from his neck and sat up, full of resolution. But when he tried to tell her, she laid a hand across his mouth and would not listen.

"Later," she pleaded. "We cannot spoil this moment with serious talk." She scrambled to her knees. "Besides, I must now attempt to make myself respectable."

Devereux accepted temporary defeat. His eyebrow rose sardonically. "That will be no easy task, my love. There is a total absence of facilities for you to make your toilet. And as for the remnants of that extraordinary costume . . ."

"I shall contrive," she declared blithely.

"Then I shall await the result with keen anticipation."

He stretched out on the bed and propped his head on

his sound arm so that he might watch her. "You realize, my dear love, that your father is going to demand nothing less that my head on the end of a pole for involving you in all this—not to mention the added provocation of having his daughter restored to him in the guise of something between a player from the Comédie Française and a back-alley doxy!"

Madalena giggled. "But you did not involve me," she pointed out, becoming rather flustered, as, under his amused gaze, she struggled to wrap her shirt as far over as possible before pushing it firmly into her breeches. "I involved myself."

"Very true, *mignonne*—but I doubt that argument will carry sufficient weight with your irate parent."

"Oh, Papa is not like that! He knows his daughter too well."

"I trust you may be right."

Madalena was studying the jerkin with a furrowed brow. "Do you think your brigand friend might have a piece of leather thonging? It is just possible that he may use it sometimes to secure his victims."

She stared at him as he laughed aloud. "What is so funny?"

"You are, my dear love—funny and incredible and quite wonderful! Do you realize that most young ladies would by now be prostrate in such a situation—and you talk prosaically of thonging!"

She grinned. *"Eh bien!* I am not so feeble as that!"

"You are not feeble at all." Her resilience was a revelation to him, as was everything about her. He wondered briefly if in ten years, twenty years from now, she would still be a source of new delights.

A great commotion outside drew them both to the window. A carriage was hurtling down the track, with little Frochot up on the box, brandishing a driving whip and noisily urging on a superbly matched pair of blood horses.

He slewed the equipage around into the courtyard with hair-raising skill, and it passed from their view.

"Now, what's that old devil up to?" Devereux mused, frowning. "He didn't come by a turnout like that honestly, I'll be bound."

He reached the bedroom door just as the outer door was thrown open, in time to see several of the men bundling in a tall, elegant and quite unmistakable figure.

"Samson! Good God, man—what is all this?"

The black man was somehow managing to preserve an air of unruffled dignity despite the business end of a musket that rested just below his left ear.

"Monsieur! So we were right to suspect you were in trouble."

Le Loup-garou heard this exchange of pleasantries with the air of a small boy about to have yet another prize toy snatched from his eager grasp. "You know this black pig, *mon vieux?*" he muttered.

"Certainly I know him. Release him at once."

Reluctantly the musket was lowered; Samson moved it aside and stepped forward.

"We were troubled when you did not come. Madame sent me with the carriage in case you had met with an accident."

"Ah, that explains the carriage," said Devereux. His eyes rested for a moment on Madalena, and then he said with apparent casualness, "The gentleman you were expecting? Did he arrive safely?"

Samson inclined his head. "Yes, monsieur. All is well. He awaits your arrival."

Hope hovered uncertainly in Madalena's face. Devereux drew her into the circle of his arm. "Yes, *chérie*—your father is safe. You will see him very soon now." She nodded, unable to speak. He turned to Samson. "You come most opportunely with the carriage; mademoiselle may now be driven in comfort."

The brigand chief looked less than pleased, however;

to lose two prisoners *and* a fine carriage and pair took some swallowing. When, however, the situation was explained to him, he bowed to the inevitable. The name of Monsieur de Brussec was not unknown even here, so far from Paris; he even went so far as to offer them an escort so that the little mademoiselle's papa might be safely restored to her.

The offer was tactfully refused, but the big man said cheerfully that they would be close at hand if needed—and the werewolf and young mademoiselle parted on the best of terms.

Several hours later, the carriage was turning in between the high ornamental gates of Madame de Marron's villa and drawing to a halt before the steps. Madalena had been very silent on the journey, and Devereux, sensing that she was suffering from a degree of reaction, made no attempt to rouse her. She attributed his apparent withdrawal to discomfort and weariness and pretended to sleep so that he would not feel obliged to entertain her. Little by little, a black depression settled upon her.

In the foyer, Janine de Marron waited; her eyes met Devereux's, the fine line of her brows arching in amused query at the sight of the wraithlike little figure at his side.

There was a stirring in the doorway behind her, and the small figure came to life suddenly, to run and fling herself upon the astonished gentleman who had emerged.

Monsieur de Brussec caught Madalena in a bearlike embrace, his strong, intellectual face working with emotion.

"Maddie! My little Maddie! Why are you here? I could not believe my eyes when I looked from the window!"

Madalena was laughing and crying at once; her explanations became increasingly incoherent, until her father cried enough. "Later, *ma fille!* For now, I think you should go with madame." He looked enquiringly at Janine. "Mayhap she can transform you into something less resembling a little scarecrow?"

Introductions were effected and Janine came forward with outstretched hands. "Indeed yes, *chérie*." With droll good humor she measured Madalena's slight frame against her own more voluptuous curves. "*Hélas,* it will not be easy, but my good Celestine will contrive something."

"You are very kind, madame," Madalena said in a flat, polite voice. Her heightened senses had at once detected the degree of intimacy between this woman and Dev; like Lady Serena, she was of his world. The notion left her curiously bereft. Her big adventure was ended.

"And when you have her safe in a dress, my dear Janine," Dev was declaring firmly, "you may burn those damned breeches!"

"Oh, no!" cried Madalena. "I am very fond of my breeches."

"Well, I am not, child." Dev took her chin between finger and thumb and shook it gently; a smile lurked deep in his eyes. "They seem destined to land you in trouble —and I do not propose to spend the rest of my days hauling you out of scrapes."

"Oh, well . . ." She swallowed hard and allowed herself to be led away by a vastly intrigued Janine. Dev had never looked at her in just such a way!

Devereux also found himself coming under keen scrutiny from another direction. Monsieur de Brussec had intercepted that same look, and was, not unnaturally, curious to learn its meaning—and to learn also how his daughter, who should have been safe with her aunt in England, came instead to be gallivanting across France in so unseemly a fashion and in the company of this strange and enigmatic character, Lytten.

"I believe, duke," he said, somwhat sternly, "that I must demand of you an explanation." He eyed the other's arm. "Do you feel well enough to accommodate me now?"

"By all means, monsieur." Devereux sighed, stifling his by now abominable weariness.

They retired together into the front salon, where, over a glass of Janine's fine Manzanilla, he recounted as much of the affair as he thought would satisfy Monsieur de Brussec, glossing over certain episodes in deference to parental sensitivity.

His feeling for Madalena, however, was implicit in every word he spoke, and it troubled the older man greatly; no matter how many fine qualities this Lytten might possess, instinct told him that he was not a man on whom one would wish to bestow one's daughter. For the moment, though, the situation must remain in abeyance, for the conversation had turned to the matter of his own deliverance.

"For the instigation of which, I believe, I must look to you, duke," Monsieur de Brussec observed dryly. "I am bound to state that it was accomplished much against my wishes." He shrugged. "But my opinion was not heeded."

"How were matters resolved in the end, sir?"

"Oh, I believe the emperor was induced by the concerted advice of his ministers to sign my release, on the understanding that I would leave the country. It needed only a hint of mob revolt and the imminence of full-scale insurrection for him to capitulate. How much truth there was in such rumors is a matter for conjecture, but the last thing our good emperor wants at present is trouble at home."

"The rumors were true enough, monsieur, I give you my word," said Devereux. "I think you underestimate the extent of your popularity."

The lawyer smiled faintly. "Perhaps. Certainly, when I left La Force, the Rue Roi de Sicile was choked by a noisy mob. I was urged to deliver a short speech assuring them that I was a free man. From thence, my departure was discreetly engineered by the Prince De Bénévent— again, as I believe, at your instigation."

He spread his hands, and there was an air of acute

distress in the simple gesture. "So—you behold me now, duke, an exile from this land I so love."

"Not for long, monsieur, and then France will have great need of you, and men like you." Devereux drained his glass and stood up. "And now, if you would excuse me . . ."

"I must crave one moment more, if you will bear with me," said the lawyer with gentle significance. "I would be grateful to have certain matters clarified concerning my daughter. . . ."

Chapter 15

THE *Seamew* SLIPPED quietly in on a full tide, and Jason, still nursing a thick head, clambered onto the little jetty under the lee of the cliff and made fast the mooring ropes.

Devereux had been urged by Janine de Marron to stay longer and rest. Monsieur de Brussec was not now a wanted man, so what need was there for haste?

Samson had dressed the duke's wound and had confided to madame that it was still far from healed; in fact, he wondered that monseigneur should be on his feet at all. The signs of strain were plain for all to behold—the mouth set in a rigid line, the manner taciturn.

Yet he would not be shifted from his purpose. He was in a fever of impatience to be home; at home it would be easier to get Madalena to himself and talk to her, for it was becoming increasingly clear to him that she was deliberately avoiding his company.

At first he had made excuses for her: she was exhausted by her ordeal, she had much time to make up with her father. But when, by the second evening of their stay, matters had not improved, he was forced to the conclusion that the answer lay in none of these things.

She had come downstairs to dine—a vision in palest gold tiffany, so far removed from his little urchin boy that he knew a momentary stab of pure anguish. She had been quiet throughout dinner, unnaturally so for her, and afterward had hardly left her father's side.

Janine had come to lean over the back of the sofa where Devereux sat, his gaze straying often to the newly washed and gleaming red-gold curls bent so close to the graying head.

"She is an enchanting child, *chéri,*" Janine murmured. "The best thing that has ever happened to you."

"Why, so I think," he had agreed softly.

"You would marry her?"

"It is my intention to do so—if she will have me."

Janine had looked thoughtful. "You have her complete adoration. It is there for all to see whenever she speaks of you. . . ."

"And yet?" He snapped the question at her, sensing a hesitance.

Janine shrugged. "I am not sure; mayhaps the little one is just tired."

That was when he had decided. He had entrusted the safe delivery of Prince Talleyrand's letter to Janine's care and had resolved to leave on the following day.

Since it was obvious that he was in no condition to sail the boat, and Jason was still suffering severe bouts of pain, Janine had lent them Samson, who had surprised Devereux yet again by proving himself a most accomplished sailor.

He it was who now came forward to assist Madalena and her father from the boat. The sharpness of the morning air caused Madalena to wrap her cloak more closely about her.

"We'll take the passage, Jason. Fetch a lamp, will you?" Devereux turned to Monsieur de Brussec. "I fear you may find it a trifle dark and damp, monsieur, but it will save you a long and tiresome climb."

They had almost reached the mouth of the passage when a shout made them turn.

Daniel Merchent had emerged unnoticed from the shadow of the cliff near the steps, the pistol in his hand trained unwaveringly on them.

"I knew you must come, sooner or later; quite a touching family scene," he sneered.

Devereux signed to them all to stay quite still. "I had hoped you would be in custody by now, Merchent," he said evenly.

"Yes, damn you—and I very nearly was, thanks to that accursed brother of yours, Madalena, my dear! In fact, the dragoons are most probably scouring Kent for me at this very moment. But I had a score to settle here."

Madalena stared at him as at a stranger. Gone was all elegance, all charm; Daniel was now disheveled, his coat torn apart by brambles; his eyes were bloodshot and shifted constantly from one to the other of them. She was very much afraid of what he might do in this mood.

"Daniel!" she pleaded with him, and her voice shook. "You are being very silly. Please to put away your gun."

"Be quiet, you stupid little bitch!" he spat at her. "Can't you understand? It's you who have brought me to this— you, and that whey-faced brother of yours!" The gun trembled in his hand. "God! How I wanted you! I endangered my whole enterprise because of you . . . and now I'm ruined!"

At her side, Monsieur de Brussec stiffened, but Madalena laid a warning hand on his arm.

Devereux said heavily, "All this will do you no good,

Merchent. It isn't like the last time you killed here on
these cliffs. Leclerc was but one man. We are many."

Daniel frowned. "Leclerc? Oh, the little scarface. Yes,
I had to kill him. He recognized me, you see . . . saw
me in France . . . saw too much altogether. Couldn't
have him blabbing to you. But you found out anyway,
curse you!"

"Yes, I did. I know all about you now—and so do
others. That's why you can't win. You can only kill one
of us, and you haven't a hope of getting clear."

"Where would I go?" Daniel's voice was rising to the
edge of hysteria. They realized that he had gone a little
mad. "Everything is over for me, thanks to your accursed
meddling! But I can take one of you with me. Who shall
it be, Lytten? You . . . or your beloved Madalena?"

He swung the gun on Madalena as he spoke. There was
a deafening explosion, and she felt a tremendous impact
as she fell. In the noise and confusion, it took her several
moments to realize that she was not shot at all, but that
Dev had hurled himself upon her and thrown her to the
ground as the shot was fired.

It was Daniel who lay dead in a crumpled heap. Armand came from the passageway with one of the manor
servants, very shaken and holding in his hand a still-
smoking pistol. He threw it down in disgust and stumbled
forward to embrace his father.

"I was almost too late, Papa," he stammered through
chattering teeth. "I thought Dan was captured, and then I
saw him as I was taking an early ride. He was in the
bushes, watching the boat out in the bay. I knew at once
what must be his intention, and I had no weapon. So I
rode to the manor for a pistol, and Thomas here showed
me the way through the tunnel so that I might arrive in
time to warn you."

Madalena scarcely heard his words; she was on her
knees beside Dev. He was lying frighteningly still and

ashen-faced, his greatcoat thrown off in his fall, and blood was seeping steadily through his bandages.

She raised her face, distraught with grief, to her papa. *"Il est mort!"* she sobbed.

The lawyer bent to look, but Samson was already kneeling at her side. "No, mademoiselle." His quiet voice was reassuring. "He lives."

" 'Tis the fall opened up his wound," grunted Jason. "Best get him up to the house. I'll go for the doctor."

"No . . . no, I will go," said Armand. "I can go more quickly, and you will be of more use to stay here."

Samson lifted the duke with ease, and the party hurried through the tunnel in silence. Jason's lamp bobbed ahead of them all the while, and Madalena, with tears coursing soundlessly down her cheeks, was obliged to run in order to keep abreast of Samson's loping strides.

In the master bedchamber at the manor, Dr. Laidlaw dressed the wound and rebandaged it, and Armand, who had been assisting him, moved over to the fireplace, where his father and the rest were holding a subdued inquest on the recent happenings.

Above their heads hung a portrait of the duchess. Madalena remembered it from her previous visit to this room—a younger, more vivacious duchess than she had known, but with the same smile of incredible sweetness. She found her gaze returning to it again and again, as though silently entreating her help.

Dr. Laidlaw was now feeling Dev's pulse, his face grave. Madalena hovered at his shoulder, and a great fear was growing in her.

"When I removed the bullet," she whispered, "did I do something wrong?"

The doctor laid the arm back on the bed and turned to give her his whole attention. "When *you* removed the bullet?"

She nodded. "You were . . . so grim. I wondered . . ." Tightness closed her throat completely.

"I thought it was your brother who aspired to be the doctor!" Dr. Laidlaw smiled and gave her hand a comforting pat. "You did a splendid job, my dear child! By God's grace, the lung is not affected, and I have every hope that the duke will make a full recovery. This is but a setback."

"You are sure? *Dieu!* He has such pallor!"

"The wound was torn open; his grace has lost a deal more blood, mademoiselle. He should not have been gallivanting about." The doctor shook his head. "These strong, silent men—they convince themselves that they are indestructible."

"It was for me," she breathed on a sob, and he found his curiosity growing by the minute.

The duke's eyes fluttered open, and Madalena was at his side in an instant, bending over him, smoothing back his hair.

"Still there . . . little Madonna?" The murmured words were scarcely audible.

"Oui, bien-aimé!"

He possessed himself of her hand. "Will you be there always?"

"As long as you have need of me," she vowed steadily. "Now, you must sleep."

His eyes closed, and with Madalena's hand still held prisoner, he slept.

Dr. Laidlaw, as the only close witness to the little scene, found a great many things suddenly made clear.

Madalena and her father were embraced with great volubility by Mrs. Vernon on their arrival. Relief struggled with tears and recriminations as she declared that she had sustained a severe shock to her system in the past week, with first Armand and then Madalena disappearing without apparent trace. Had her dear children not remained at home to sustain her, she must have endured far worse!

The brigadier had been summoned from Lower Meckleton and had taken himself off at once to London with Kit to see what could be done to discover their whereabouts. It was only when Kit returned with Armand that they had learned something of what had been happening.

Armand's belief that Madalena had gone to France with Lytten to secure his papa's release had brought on fresh palpitations, but his aunt's attention had soon been diverted to horrified contemplation of Daniel Merchent's duplicity—and of what an escape Madalena had had, if only she might be brought safely home to appreciate it.

Trying though he found her, Monsieur de Brussec bore his sister-in-law's empty prattle with patience and an innate courtesy. He assured her of his deep gratitude for all the love and care she had bestowed upon his incorrigible pair.

Incorrigible or not, he was patently overjoyed to be once again united with his children. He received the intelligence that his son wished to practice medicine with quiet pleasure. Armand had already confessed to his papa the extent of his involvement in Daniel's smuggling activities, and had been surprised by the mildness of his reproof.

His father was, in fact, far more troubled by the inconsistency of his daughter's behavior. For several days Madalena could hardly be persuaded to leave the duke's bedside—until the morning when she and her papa had arrived, to be greeted by a beaming Thomas with the news that the patient was very much improved and was demanding to see her. To everyone's astonishment, she had turned pale and rushed from the house.

She would not be persuaded to return. When her father had sought her out later, he found her tearful but adamant.

"You are not being very consistent, *chérie*," he had probed gently. "When the duke is so ill, you can scarcely be prised from his side. Now, you will not go near him. He is understandably distressed—and bewildered!"

Fresh tears sprang to her eyes, but she said nothing.

Monsieur de Brussec had continued with a touch of

wry humor, "When a gentleman has made up his mind to propose, it is very lowering to find his beloved so elusive! The more so when he is confined—and so may not seek her out!"

He surprised in her a look of acute misery.

"You do not understand, Papa. . . . I cannot . . . he must not . . ."

It was impossible to explain, even to Papa. It had started even before they had arrived back in England— with Madame de Marron, in fact.

"Such an adventure, my love!" she had sighed enviously. "And you may depend upon it, Dev will marry you after this. It cannot be otherwise—I see all the signs. Ah, how you are fortunate, to succeed where so many of us have tried and failed!"

"No!" Madalena had said flatly to an astounded madame.

And now, since she had arrived back in England, it had never stopped. Not only was Papa positively encouraging the match; Tante Esmé, too, had quite taken for granted that she and Dev would marry as soon as he was recovered. In her code of conduct, one did not disappear with a gentleman to spend several days alone in his company. But if the worst happened, then marriage was the only possible outcome. Her head was already full of Easter bridals—such a delightful time for a wedding!

Even Kit seemed to have accepted the inevitability of their union. Phoebe shared her mother's view, though she also thought the whole affair prodigiously romantic, and went on and on about it until Madalena was driven from the house.

It was on just such an occasion that she was walking, head down, when a carriage drew abreast of her and stopped.

Dr. Laidlaw eyed the drooping figure with concern and a degree of bewilderment. "Good day to you, mademoiselle. Do I find you well?"

"Oh, yes. I thank you," came the listless reply.

"Well, you do not look it, if I may say so!" the doctor observed in his gruff, homely way. "You have been neglecting your patient of late."

Delicate color stained her cheeks. "I . . ." Her eyes went to his face, and the question seemed to be forced from her. "How is he?"

Those speaking eyes conveyed so much that her words did not. He weighed his own words with care. "I am a little concerned . . ."

"He is not ill again?" There was panic in her voice now. "No one has said anything to me! Armand visited only this morning, and he did not say—"

"Perhaps, mademoiselle, he thought you would not care to know?"

She waited to hear no more. Her feet were flying over the ground in the direction of the manor, and the doctor looked after her with a satisfied smile.

Young Thomas, opening the door to Madalena, gaped as she rushed past without a word, taking the stairs at an unladylike two at a time. At the door of the bedchamber she paused to regain her breath.

Samson answered her knock. He had stayed on until he was able to take home a satisfactory report to madame. His face now split in a huge grin. "Mademoiselle! Come in. You will be welcome."

She stepped past him, and the door closed softly, leaving her alone. She took a few uncertain steps toward the bed. It was empty.

"I am over here, Madalena."

Devereux was in the big leather armchair near the fireplace, a fur rug across his knees. He wore a handsome brocade dressing robe, but though the light from the window fell on a face that was pale against the crimson cushions, and his arm was still in a sling, his eyes were clear and curiously bright.

"You are not worse!" she cried indignantly.

"I am desolated to disappoint you, child," he drawled.

Madalena stood poised for flight, her heavy blue cloak held close about her, the hood, as ever, slipping back. As he watched her, his lips twisted in that self-denigrating sarcasm, as once before when she had hurt him deeply. "So? Finding me thus lamentably on the road to recovery, will you now rush away again? I should like to know what I have done."

"I . . . you have done nothing." She swallowed miserably, and added in a whisper, "It is what I fear you might feel constrained to do."

"And what is that, pray?"

Scarlet with embarrassment, Madalena crossed to the window and stared out, very conscious of his bright blue eyes boring into her back.

"Come, *ma mie.*" The words grated slightly. "You have never dissembled with me until now."

She swung around, her eyes flitting briefly to the portrait above his head, as though she would draw courage from it. "You are right. I have been a big coward, when it needs only a little resolution." Her voice held the flatness of despair.

"Everyone says you must marry me because I have compromised myself with you, but it is not at all necessary, *je t'assure!* It is not your fault that I came to France . . . and I do not care if they all think that I have been your *jolie fille de joie!* So . . . you need not concern yourself . . ."

So that was it! In his relief he almost laughed aloud, and mentally consigned all well-meaning busybodies to the devil! He sensed that he must tread carefully if he would convince her.

"Have you ever known me to care what people say of me?"

"No." She faltered. "But this concerns me also . . . and because of what happened in France . . . and because you have respect for Papa, you might feel an obligation . . ."

"And I do not need to. Is that what you are saying?"

"Yes. I will make Papa see . . ."

He pressed her. "You find perhaps that you are not in love with me, after all?"

"I did not say that!" The cry was wrung from her. She drew a quivering breath. "But I will not be your wife to satisfy stupid conventions—or to preserve my good name, for which I care nothing!"

"That sounds very final, *ma chère*," Devereux said softly. "So. You will not be my wife. What, then, will you be?"

Madalena's lashes were spiked with tears; through them his face was splintering into a thousand glittering pieces.

"I will be anything you wish, for as long as you wish . . . but, oh . . . I did not give myself to you so that I might entrap you into marriage, and I would not have you think it. . . ." She choked to a halt and turned abruptly to the window again.

"Oh, good God!" Devereux exploded, unsure whether to laugh or be furiously angry. "Come here, you absurd infant!"

But she would only shake her head, her back set resolutely against him. Not for the first time he cursed his stupid, lingering weakness, unsure whether his legs would carry him as far as the window.

"Will you put me to the trouble of fetching you?"

The grim determination in his voice brought her around. He was already folding back the rug. In a flash she was across the space between them, and found herself held, and inexorably drawn forward.

"You cannot . . . you must not attempt . . . Your arm . . ."

"Be quiet!" ordered the duke in un-lover-like tones, and proceeded to kiss her with a thoroughness that belied his infirmity. When at length he was satisfied, Madalena was somehow sitting upon his knee in a tangle of blue cloak, firmly held by his good arm.

"It was a trick!" she reproached him.

"But of course, my dearest love! At our very first encounter, I warned you that I seldom play fair. Whatever gave you the notion that I would do so now?"

"*Dieu!* Do you remember so far back?"

"I remember everything concerning you," he said softly.

"Oh!" She went pink and buried her head blissfully against his shoulder. Devereux lovingly removed a red curl that was tickling his chin, and endeavored to see her face.

"Would you really come to me?" he demanded of her. "On any terms that I might dictate?"

"But of course!" came the muffled reply. "Have I not said?"

"You have talked a great deal of nonsense," he said forcibly. "Well, you shall have my terms, and we shall see how well you abide by your words." He paused. "I will accept nothing less than marriage, mademoiselle, and a lifetime of devotion. There—what have you to say to that?"

She lifted her head slowly, and in her eyes, uncertainty struggled with a growing rapture. "*Voyons!* Is that really what you wish?"

"I have set my heart on it, *mignonne.*"

"You prefer me to Lady Serena?" she persisted.

"Good God! Why ever should I want to marry Serena?"

Madalena considered, trying very hard to be objective. "She would be a very good kind of wife for you, I think. She is of the world, and moves in the very best circles . . . and then, she is also of good birth and knows all the right people. Or there is Madame de Marron, of course. . . ."

Devereux stopped her mouth in the only possible way, pausing just once in order to remove his arm from its sling.

"Tiens! You must not. What are you thinking of?"

He raised his hand with infinite care and loosened the clasp of her cloak. "I am getting rid of this damned encumbrance!"

"But your shoulder!" Madalena wailed.

"To the devil with my shoulder. What do I care for that, when I am afflicted by a far more grievous malady."

Madalena's breath caught in sudden fear. Had Dr. Laidlaw not hinted at something . . . ?

"Ah, *mon amour,* tell me!" she cried. "Is it very bad?"

His eyes lifted briefly to his mother's portrait. Then he took one of her small hands and slid it inside his robe, placing it just above his heart so that she could feel it hammering.

"There," he murmured gravely. "You see how it is with me. And it is only fair to warn you, *ma chère* Madalena, that there is no possibility of a cure!"

About the Author

Sheila Walsh lives with her husband in Southport, Lancashire, England, and is the mother of two daughters. She began to seriously think about writing when a local writers' club was formed. After experimenting with short stories and plays, she completed her first novel, THE GOLDEN SONGBIRD, which subsequently won her an award in 1974 presented by the Romantic Novelists' Association. MADALENA is her second novel; both are published by NAL.